THEY C

Wild Bill Hickok—In a town running wild he was the peacemaker of last resort, the man whose guns blazed all the law that was needed to bring a deadly order. And each day brought more men daring to call him out.

Elliot Carson—He came from the East with fierce ambitions for a new life, but his hard-driving crusade for truth brought him some powerful enemies.

Connie Witherspoon—She held her head high against the public stigma of a bitter divorce but privately fought to open herself to the new man who was trying to win her love.

Jim Mulrey—A blood-crazed avenger, he haunted the shadows of Abilene, nervously awaiting the right moment to gun down his sworn enemy, Bill Hickok.

The Stagecoach Series
Ask your bookseller for the books you have missed

STAGECOACH STATION 10:

ABILENE

Hank Mitchum

 Created by the producers of
**Wagons West, White Indian,
Saga of the Southwest,** and
The Kent Family Chronicles Series.

Executive Producer: Lyle Kenyon Engel

BANTAM BOOKS
TORONTO · NEW YORK · LONDON · SYDNEY

STAGECOACH STATION #10: ABILENE

*A Bantam Book / published by arrangement with
Book Creations, Inc.*

Bantam edition / February 1984

*Produced by Book Creations, Inc.
Executive Producer: Lyle Kenyon Engel.*

ISBN 0-553-23858-2

Published simultaneously in the United States and Canada

PRINTED IN THE UNITED STATES OF AMERICA

O   0 9 8 7 6 5 4 3 2 1

Author's Note

This book is a work of fiction; however, many incidents really happened and many of the characters existed.

Abilene, Kansas, was established in 1858, but not until 1867 did it become a shipping point for cattle being herded north from Texas along the Chisholm Trail. By 1871, Abilene was reaching maturity as a cattle town, but by then the prosperity its citizens enjoyed from the thousands of cowboys passing through was tainted by the senseless violence, indiscreet behavior, and property damage that accompanied each trail herd.

Despite an abysmal record of murder and mayhem, and despite rising pressure from local farmers and businessmen, no one was able to keep law and order in Abilene, since there were no town officials whose job it was to do so. But by the spring of 1870, the mayhem, vice, and unrestrained good times had risen to such a dangerous crescendo that the townspeople were finally pushed beyond the point of tolerance. Elections were held, and those elected were directed to take action. They in turn called upon men brave enough to put a lid on this seething caldron.

One of those men was James Butler "Wild Bill" Hickok.

STAGECOACH STATION 10:

ABILENE

Chapter 1

The stagecoach from Omaha was not yet within sight of Abilene, and Sue Ann Mobley was restless. A small, pert, pretty young thing, with thick auburn curls and dark brown eyes with heavy, seductive lashes, she could not have been much over eighteen, if she was that. She had the feverish, almost giddy air of one who has burnt all her bridges behind her and, as a result, is not sure if she should clap her hands and dance with delight—or cry.

Sue Ann was seated with the two other female passengers on the most comfortable bench inside the stage—with their backs to the driver—where the discomforts of dust and rain were least. Sighing impatiently, she pulled aside the shade and leaned out the side window. She had learned by now to expect nothing from the view but the usual, interminable sweep of Kansas prairie, and she was for this reason amazed when she was greeted instead with a very different sight—ahead of the stage was a long column of slow-moving cattle.

It was a spectacle indeed, and her cry of delight instantly alerted the other six passengers. What they saw was the long line of cattle called a trail herd winding up and over the distant hills like a great snake, its head unseen somewhere over the rolling prairie that lay

1

before them and its tail out of sight well behind them. Over this immense procession of livestock hung a spreading cloud of dust, which before long began drifting into the coach's interior.

The stagecoach, keeping to the roadway, soon was much closer to the trail herd, and the passengers were able to watch as cowboys, their bandannas pulled up over their noses to protect them from the choking dust, galloped back and forth along the flanks of the herd. With stinging flicks from their ropes, they kept the cattle moving, and occasionally their Indian-like yells could be heard above the ceaseless rattle of the stagecoach.

Before long the stage was near enough to the trail herd for the passengers to hear the muffled cracking of the cows' ankle joints, the steady thudding of hooves, and the sharp clacking of long horns swinging against each other. And all the while the dust got thicker.

Ducking her head back into the stage, Sue Ann slumped against her seat, holding up her hand to protect her face from the thickening dust. Following her example, Major Horace Farber—sitting alone on the center bench with his back against one of the doors and his legs straddling the seat—took a handkerchief from his frock-coat pocket and held it over his nose and mouth. The other passengers immediately took similar precautions, and Sue Ann, looking around at the half-masked faces of the coach's occupants, found their darting eyes vaguely amusing.

Sue Ann wasn't about to let a little dust dampen her spirits. After all, with every mile she was putting distance between herself and her home—and her father, with whom she could no longer bear to live. When her cousin, during a trip south, had written of the excitement in the burgeoning town of Abilene—the glittering night life, the flourishing businesses, and the abun-

2

dance of men—Sue Ann took what money she had managed to save and bought the first stage ticket south. But the letter had not mentioned the dust, noise, and danger brought by the trail herds, which were responsible for Abilene's prosperity.

The fierce Texas longhorn that roamed unclaimed in the southern part of Texas was worth only three to four dollars in its own territory, but buyers in big cities to the north—Chicago or St. Louis—paid up to forty dollars a head. Since no railroad ran through Texas, cattlemen herded the longhorns north into Kansas, Colorado, and Missouri—even as far north as Cheyenne, Wyoming—where their herds could be loaded onto railroad cars and shipped to the buyers who would pay top dollar.

Sue Ann watched the powerful beasts thunder past the coach and marveled at the seemingly endless number of them.

"My goodness," she said, "if we get any closer to that herd, it will swallow us up! Are we going to ride straight on through it?"

"It sure does look that way, don't it," said Mike Williams, the young man sitting in the corner across from Sue Ann. "My! Look at the way them cowboys ride! Like they was born to the saddle. Bet this is a herd that's come up from Texas."

"Texans, are they? . . . Well, they certainly do yell a lot," replied Sue Ann.

"Just like Comanches," Mike agreed eagerly, glancing out the window as one hard-riding Texan swept past. " 'Course that's because the Texans have had to deal with the Comanche for some time now. They've had a real war with them for close to twenty years."

"That war's done," commented Elliot Carson, the tall gentleman sitting in the middle of the bench, next to Mike. "The Comanche are finished."

3

"Maybe," said Mike, "but not the Apache, I'll bet. No, not them."

Elliot Carson did not say any more. He just nodded amiably to Mike, then looked past him out the window at the tide of longhorns that appeared ready at any moment to engulf the still-moving stage.

Elliot Carson was a tall, lean-faced fellow with warm brown eyes, a shock of auburn hair, sideburns, and a mustache. He had a ready smile and had given everyone in the stage the impression that despite the tedium of the ride, he was greatly excited by this trip west and was looking forward eagerly to its adventures.

This impression was an accurate one, though it did not begin to tell the whole story. Eager for adventure though Elliot was, he was no headstrong fool plunging in without a proper evaluation of the waters below. He had a sharp intellect and a native Vermonter's wary, inbred caution. He had a job—and a good one—awaiting him in Abilene. In his early thirties, fresh from a Vermont daily, he was about to take on his new post as managing editor of the *Abilene Chronicle*.

Having already read much about Abilene's lawlessness, he was anxious to see the notorious trail town for himself. Being the editor of a newspaper in such a town would certainly not be boring work, and it was not lost on Elliot, ambitious as he was, that Mark Twain first made his reputation when he was a reporter in the raw and untamed West. Secretly harboring a hope for the same recognition for himself, Elliot was looking forward to interviewing James Butler "Wild Bill" Hickok, the town's marshal, as soon as he got settled in Abilene. He was hoping to write an article good enough to be accepted by the prestigious *Atlantic Monthly* in Boston, the editor of which he had already written concerning it.

Meanwhile, Elliot regarded Mike Williams—the excitable young man sitting beside him—with much the same curiosity as he did Abilene and its famous marshal. For as Elliot was quite well aware, Mike Williams was more eager to meet Wild Bill Hickok than was Elliot himself. Mike had already confided to Elliot that his sole purpose in journeying to Abilene was to become one of Wild Bill Hickok's deputies. But even if Mike had not told him, Elliot would have been able to guess the truth. In direct imitation of the gunfighter, Mike Williams had let his long sandy hair grow out so that it fell clear to his shoulders. Stuck into his belt—butts out—he wore two pearl-handled Remington Frontier .44s, and on his upper lip he had grown a long, drooping mustache—a rather pale imitation of the mustache favored by Wild Bill.

The young man's conscious aping of his hero would have struck Elliot Carson as comical had it not been for the grave sincerity in Mike's wide blue eyes. Reflecting on the matter during this long ride, Elliot had come to the conclusion that Mike Williams was just as sincere as any raw recruit enlisting in the U.S. Cavalry. As those innocents saw it, they were offering their lives and sacred honor to defeat the barbarian hordes hampering the advance of Western civilization. Only in the case of Wild Bill and his beleaguered deputies, those barbarian hordes were cowboys from Texas, the very same young men now galloping back and forth outside the stage.

Elliot had read several issues of the Abilene newspaper, sent to him by its publisher, and in each one were accounts of the young town's troubles with the Texas cowboys fresh off the long Chisholm Trail. Their minds dulled and their bodies worn by the grueling trip north on horseback, the cowboys looked forward to Abilene as the end of their responsibilities and the beginning of their pleasures. While the owners of Abilene's saloons, dance halls, and brothels welcomed the cowboys—or Texans, as they were called—the farmers and merchants, ministers and grocers dreaded their arrival, for murder and mayhem inevitably resulted.

Elliot recalled the headline of one newspaper editorial: "Hell Is Now In Session" it read and was followed by an outraged account of the seventeen murders Abilene had hosted during the previous six months. Few towns in Vermont could offer a newspaperman the exciting opportunities Abilene promised, Elliot thought, as he glanced over at Sue Ann, still looking out the window—but what would it offer a young woman like her?

The stagecoach lurched to a halt so abruptly that Mike Williams was nearly catapulted across the center bench and into Sue Ann's lap. Elliot Carson swiftly reached up to grab hold of the overhead strap and leaned over, sticking his head out the window to see what was wrong.

It was precisely as Sue Ann had suggested a moment before. The stage was hemmed in by bawling, confused longhorns, while from his perch atop the stage, the driver unfurled a series of scalding curses at the Texas cowboys and their cattle.

Connie Witherspoon, the woman sitting in the other corner of Sue Ann's bench, looked with some concern at Agnes Thatcher, the older woman sitting between them.

"Isn't this dangerous?" Connie asked. "What if these animals stampede?"

"Hush," the older woman said with a nervous smile. "You'll give the cattle ideas."

Connie smiled slightly at the older woman's comment, then, her anger barely concealed, she said, "How could they hear me above the roar of that intemperate stage driver? I don't know why he is howling so. It is his fault we are in this pretty mess. Surely, from his

6

perch, he must have been able to see the cattle. You don't suppose he's drunk again, do you?"

Elliot smiled at the woman's remark; he understood perfectly her frustration. The driver was doing nothing but swear a blue streak at the cattle, which by this time were nudging heavily at the sides of the coach, causing it to rock slightly.

"I wouldn't worry, Miss Witherspoon," Elliot said. "I am sure the cowboys in charge of these cattle will have us out of this in no time."

"Maybe I better get out and see what I can do," said Mike Williams, his hand moving toward the door handle.

Reaching out quickly, Elliot prevented Mike from pushing open the door. "I wouldn't do that," he cautioned.

"Well, someone's got to do something."

"But not you."

"Why not?"

"You're not mounted, that's why. You're on foot."

"Yes," said Connie Witherspoon. "You might get crushed between the stage and those milling cattle. Mr. Carson is right. You're safer in here, surely."

"Go on. Let the poor sap get out," said Jim Mulrey, the shabbily dressed man seated in the corner at Elliot's left. "He'd look just dandy with a horn in his rear."

The three women in the stage sucked in their breath at this brutal and coarse comment, and Elliot turned to face Mulrey. The little fellow was scrunched against the wall, looking over at Mike Williams with a mean, spiteful smirk on his lined face. Mulrey's generally gray complexion and small, bony frame gave Elliot the feeling that he was looking at a human-sized rat. And Elliot was well aware that Mulrey was no cleaner than one.

7

"I think perhaps you would do well to watch your language," Elliot advised him.

Mulrey turned his piercing eyes on Elliot. "This here's a free country, mister. I'll damn well say what I want to say . . . when I want to say it."

"That's all right, Mr. Carson," said Mike Williams hastily, sitting back in his seat. "I guess it would be foolish of me to leave the stage now."

"Here comes one of the cowboys," said Sue Ann.

Turning, Elliot saw a tall rider pushing his mount through the longhorns toward the stage. He was a lean, nut-brown fellow, who looked as tough as old leather and rode his horse with a skill Elliot immediately envied. As the Texan glanced about, he exhibited an assurance of command that seemed instinctive. It was obvious to Elliot that this rider must be the trail boss. Slowly, steadily, he worked his horse through the crush of milling, nervous cattle, their horns clacking, until he was within a few feet of the coach. By this time the stage driver had calmed down somewhat and was able to engage the trail boss in conversation.

"What the hell ya doin' out here—east of Abilene?" the driver exclaimed.

"Calm down, old man," the head Texan shouted back. "The stock pens are full. We're swinging around to grazing land north of town while we wait our turn."

"Damn nuisance!" the driver muttered.

"I got the herd thinned out yonder," the cowboy continued. "You just follow me through these critters."

The trail boss then rode up to the head of the stage team and began clearing the way. Other cowboys appeared then and began helping him. One of them, on his way past the stage, grinned in at Sue Ann, and without thinking, she smiled and waved back at him—at which the cowboy took off his hat and let out a whoop.

Scarlet with embarrassment, Sue Ann quickly ducked her head back into the stage. "Oh, my," she said. "I didn't mean to cause all that commotion."

"Oh, no," said Mulrey, his voice heavy with sarcasm, "of course you didn't."

Mortified, Sue Ann shrank back from the suggestive gleam in Mulrey's eyes.

Abruptly, the shouts and hoots of still more cowboys filled the stagecoach. Glancing out, Elliot saw drovers crowding in close to the stage, urging the cattle back from it with Comanche-like shouts and cruel snaps from their ropes. Other cowboys continued on past the stage, joining those who had already positioned themselves ahead of it.

The stagecoach groaned and began to move forward once again. It was as though the coach were at sea and these horsemen were pulling it through the water after them. Slowly, ever so slowly, the coach gained speed, and at last it pulled free of the herd. Then the crack of the driver's whip sounded above the bawling of the cattle, and the stagecoach lurched forward. In a matter of minutes, it was once more moving at full speed toward Abilene.

Elliot leaned back against his seat and took a deep breath. It had been an interesting encounter—so interesting, in fact, that he had no doubt it would make a fine article for an eastern paper or magazine. Especially noteworthy was that nervous moment when those horned brutes began crowding upon the flimsy coach from all sides. Elliot began structuring the story in his mind as the coach hurtled on.

Connie Witherspoon was a mature, handsome widow in her late twenties. Tall, with somewhat gaunt cheeks, luminous brown eyes, and thick, dark hair, she had always regarded her striking beauty as a hindrance. When men saw her, they did not think of the mind that dwelt behind those lovely eyes; they thought only of what stratagems they might employ to gain access to her favors.

Still upset by Jim Mulrey's remark to Sue Ann a moment before, Connie was debating whether or not to lean over and comfort Sue Ann when Major Horace Farber, sitting directly in front of her on the middle bench, took a whiskey flask from the side pocket of his frock coat.

The major was a florid-faced gentleman in his early fifties. He had a noticeable paunch, and his cherry-red nose proclaimed him to be very fond of the bottle. His eyes were a watery blue, and his round face almost seemed cherubic. He wore a white flannel suit with a black string tie knotted at his throat, and his neat Vandyke beard—along with the bushy mane of yellowing white hair brushed straight back and falling nearly to his shoulders—did much to further enhance his appearance.

Uncapping the flask, he took a quick snort, after which, coughing slightly, he wiped his mouth with the back of his hand and then dropped the flask back into his pocket.

"Really, Major," Connie said indignantly. "This is not a public saloon."

"Ah, if only it were, my dear . . . if only it were. But soon we will finish with this miserable journey and arrive in Abilene, where as I understand it, the gaming tables flourish unrepentant and in full flower. I am hopeful that my recent ill fortunes will become a thing of the past."

Mulrey spoke up then, his mean voice cutting like a knife through the coach. "Hey there, Major, how about letting me have some of that?"

The major turned slowly to look upon Mulrey. He might have been peering at something scurrying out from under a rock. "What was that?" the major demanded. "Were you addressing me?"

"You heard me," Mulrey snapped. "The least you could do is offer me some of that whiskey! Ain't polite, drinking alone."

"You?" the major cried indignantly. "I share this flask with you? Why, sir, you are a cur! You insult young ladies and exult in the ignorance of others. I would sooner offer a drink to the devil himself. Buy your own, sir!"

"Why, you drink-sodden old fool!" rasped Mulrey. Furious, he reached in under his soiled coat, apparently for a weapon. As he did so, Mike Williams quickly drew one of his Remingtons and, cocking it, held it inches from Mulrey's face.

"Just simmer down, Mulrey," Mike said, "or this might go off."

Mulrey's face blackened with fury.

For a terrible, sickening instant Connie thought she was going to see a murder. Beside her, Agnes Thatcher gasped, but then Elliot Carson reached out, quickly pushing the Remington down. Leaning heavily on Mulrey, Elliot pinned the man into the corner. As Mike put away his gleaming revolver, Carson smiled at Mulrey, his full weight now bearing down on the smaller man.

"The major is right, you know," he told Mulrey. "You did seem to take an unseemly delight in Sue Ann's embarrassment. I am sure she had no idea that Texan was going to yell back at her like that. Think about it a minute, and see if you don't agree." All the while Elliot spoke, he continued to lean with ever more crushing pressure on Mulrey.

Gasping for breath, Mulrey cried, "All right! All right! Let up on me, dammit!"

"Of course," Elliot said, smiling easily and sitting back. "As long as you sit quietly."

"Mr. Mulrey!" Connie snapped. "I thought what you said to Sue Ann was most uncalled for. I believe you owe her an apology."

"Damn you," Mulrey spat, his voice trembling with fury. "I'll not apologize to her or to any of you. You're all milksops . . . fools! Abilene will chew you up and spit you out."

"Indeed, you are a surly rogue, mister," said the major. "I suggest you watch out yourself, or Abilene will do the same to you."

"Maybe," snapped Mulrey. "Maybe it will, but not before I send a bullet into Wild Bill Hickok, and you can tell him that's my intent, if you want. I like to have a man worry some before I do him in."

Mulrey turned to Mike Williams. "Then afterward, kid, maybe I'll see to you." He chuckled malignantly. "Think about it."

Hearing these ugly words, Connie shuddered, appalled. By this time it was clear to her that men such as Mulrey were incorrigible. There was no sense—none at all—in her or anyone else reasoning with a degenerate of this sort. And what did that tell her about the trail town they were approaching? Was she rolling toward another Sodom or Gomorrah?

The thought troubled her deeply. She sat back in her seat and glanced out at the flat prairie, letting the placid sight do what it could to quiet her troubled mind.

Connie was not sorry she was a widow, and perhaps for that sin she was being punished. Yet nothing would ever be able to convince her that anything but a beneficent providence had rid her of the husband she had wed in her innocence and lamentable ignorance. An unfeeling, insensate brute, he had done all he could do to degrade her, both in bed and before every mutual acquaintance. Knowing nothing at all of the world—appreciating no music, no poetry, no literature—he stomped with brutal efficiency on every flower he came upon. That he died in a fury, in the midst of an apoplectic fit, had been for Connie a just and merciful deliverance. And when he was gone, she likewise felt nothing but relief to be able to drop his name and use her maiden name—Witherspoon—as if their marriage had never been.

But now, rid of one tyrant, she found herself bound to another: poverty. Her only living relative was a distant cousin, Annabelle Jenson, who had offered Connie a job in the dress shop she had recently opened in Abilene. The letter that included this offer of employment had been heavy with reluctance and weary with conditions, so that it was obvious to Connie that her cousin was not at all happy to have such an unwelcome responsibility thrust upon her. But penniless and friendless, the young widow had had no choice but to accept.

Connie was aware that Elliot Carson was watching her. The man was undoubtedly interested in her, much to Connie's delight and despair. He was a handsome man, surely, and he had just handled himself with extreme courage and clearheadedness, but Connie's first concern was keeping her job with Annabelle Jenson, who obviously cared not one whit for her. Her immediate future was not going to be easy, she knew, and staying in Abilene long enough to put away a decent nest egg for herself would be even more difficult. Only after she had done that would she allow herself to think once more of men and marriage.

Meanwhile, she would simply allow Jim Mulrey to serve as a reminder of the unthinking brutality that lay below the surface in so many men's hearts.

A horrible sense of doom had frozen the very blood in Agnes Lake Thatcher's veins. The spiteful, deadly words of Jim Mulrey kept repeating themselves over and over in her mind: *Maybe . . . but not before I send a bullet into Wild Bill Hickok.*

There was nothing but cold fear in Agnes's mind. Jim Mulrey was on his way to Abilene to kill the man she knew as James Butler Hickok! Mulrey did not care who knew it, and the horrible thing was that no one could do anything to restrain him. A man could threaten to kill another and mean it, but until he made an attempt, even his victim was helpless.

She stealthily glanced at the brooding Mulrey, crouched now like an unpleasant insect in the corner of the coach. He would, of course, be no match at all for Abilene's marshal if only he would approach Wild Bill in the open, straight on. But a man such as Mulrey did not hunt others in this fashion. He would lurk in dark alleys and favor not revolvers but sawed-off shotguns.

Agnes knew the type. Her brother had died at the hands of just such a man. Was James to go the same way?

In her early forties, Agnes Lake Thatcher had been on the road for a long while. But it had not destroyed her—not yet. Her abundant hair remained as dark as midnight, her dark eyes still sparkled with life, and her figure was still very much under control. With a masterly touch gained from long years of practice, she had rouged her cheeks and applied a soft color to her full lips. She smiled often, and when she did it was obvious that her teeth were all her own and still in fine condition.

Like Connie Witherspoon, Agnes was a widow, but unlike Connie, she had loved her husband very much and treasured his memory. He had been a circus owner when they met, and it was during their brief but happy marriage that she had made the acquaintance of James Butler Hickok, now known as Wild Bill. The tall, handsome man with the pearl-handled revolvers had befriended her husband in a Denver bar after saving him from the drunken fury of a cold-eyed gambler. Later, James—as Agnes called him—had consented to her husband's pleas ánd the next afternoon had given his circus audience an impromptu shooting demonstration.

Since then, she had thought often of that big man with the narrow waist, long hair, and sad, haunted eyes, but not until after her husband had died six months before had she thought of the gunfighter in a manner that went beyond friendship.

Agnes Thatcher and her daughter had toured their successful show—the Hippo-Olympiad and Mammoth Circus—after Mr. Thatcher's untimely death, and two months ago, in July 1871, they had brought their two-ring act to Abilene. Anyone staying in the prosperous trail town that year was sure to hear the name of its famous new marshal, and after glimpsing Wild Bill in the audience the last night of the show, Agnes found her fondness for that striking man rekindled. But only now—after seeing that her circus had secured an engagement elsewhere and that the two-ring act had been modified to spotlight her daughter as its star—had she allowed herself to set out on this strange, wildly romantic journey.

Like that surly little worm slouched across from her, she too was seeking out Abilene's town marshal— only what she sought was not his death, but James Butler Hickok's hand in marriage.

Chapter 2

The stage passengers' first glimpse of Abilene was the sprawling stockyard along the eastern edge of town. After winding its way around the town to avoid the yards, the stagecoach rumbled down Abilene's broad Texas Street, the dust it churned into the air blanketing those on the wooden sidewalks. Outside Henry H. Hazlett's Farmers' and Drovers' Supply Store, farmers new to the region stood beside their wagons and watched the stage sweep past, while their gaunt young offspring stared out from under the canvas of their wagons. After rumbling beyond the town's jail, the stagecoach slowed down some and came finally to a creaking, harness-jingling halt at the express office, just down the street from the Great Western Store, a place where a cowboy could purchase boots, hats, and gents' furnishings. The markup here, as in Hazlett's, was handsome.

For a moment the passengers remained hunched in their seats, waiting for the dust to settle. The driver, exhibiting no such patience, clambered down and yanked open the coach door. With weary smiles, the passengers began to disembark, the women first. Major Farber was the first of the men to go, and he groaned some as he rose from his uncomfortable bench seat and hopped down. Elliot went next, followed by Jim Mulrey.

17

As the three men struggled past him, Mike Williams kept to his seat. Not until Jim Mulrey had finished stepping down did he rouse himself—and then he bolted up with a violent suddenness that took everyone by surprise. Hurling himself out through the door, he nearly knocked over the driver as he flung himself onto Jim Mulrey.

Sue Ann screamed as the two men, locked in combat, flung each other to the ground, just inches from her retreating skirt. Mike Williams was getting the upper hand and had begun to thrash his opponent thoroughly when Mulrey, scrambling to his feet, managed to produce a revolver. Before he could bring it up to aim, however, Mike kicked it from Mulrey's hand and then jumped onto Mulrey, again bearing the small man down to the ground.

Straddling Mulrey's supine body, Mike began a determined, methodical pounding of the man, his blows striking first one side of Mulrey's face, then the other. At last, nearly senseless, Mulrey gave up any attempt at fighting back.

"Hey, there! That's enough of that!"

The voice was high, almost feminine—yet it carried an unmistakable ring of authority. The passengers and the others running up to watch the battle turned to see Wild Bill Hickok, his long hair tumbling to his shoulders, striding through their midst. Impressively broad-shouldered, Hickok was wearing a fancy maroon vest over a white ruffled shirt, and his long, swallow-tailed coat flapped behind him with each purposeful step. Despite the dust that seemed to cover everything, his shoes were polished to a high sheen.

Reaching the two men on the ground, Hickok bent quickly and hauled Mike Williams off the nearly unconscious Mulrey. Mike tried to shake loose from Hickok's iron grip until he saw who it was that had hold of him.

Then he quieted at once, and when Hickok released his grip, Mike hastily backed away from the downed Mulrey. With evident concern, Hickok bent to inspect Mulrey. The man's face was a mess—especially his mouth. The upper lip was swollen, the bottom lip broken through. Hickok placed a gentle hand on Mulrey's shoulder and started to help him to his feet, but one look at Hickok and Mulrey's battered face was transformed into that of a cornered brute.

"Get your hands off me!" he snarled.

Wild Bill, somewhat bewildered by such a greeting, stood up and just stared at the bleeding and crazed man, who suddenly scrambled to his feet, snatched up his weapon and carpetbag, and scurried off down the street. Frowning, Hickok turned to Mike Williams. "Do you mind telling me what this was all about, young feller?"

"Are you Wild Bill Hickok?" Mike asked.

"That's what they call me."

"I knew it was you the minute I laid eyes on you!"

"I'm glad I'm so well known. Now, would you mind answering my question? Why were you and that fellow going at it with such fury? Is he a troublemaker?"

"He was one of the passengers in the coach with us," Mike replied. "He insulted Sue Ann." As he mentioned Sue Ann, he indicated her with a nod.

Hickok looked in her direction, smiled, and touched the brim of his hat to her. Then he turned back to Mike. "Looks like you showed him the error of his ways. He didn't seem a very likable sort, I must admit."

Elliot Carson stepped forward, stuck out his hand, and introduced himself. "What Mr. Williams just told you is the truth," he said as the two shook hands. "But there's a bit more to it than that."

Hurrying over, Connie Witherspoon broke into the conversation. "I think you should tell Mr. Hickok

19

now," she said. "He should know what Jim Mulrey said to us in the coach."

"I was just about to do that, Miss Witherspoon," replied Elliot.

"So was I," said Mike Williams.

Elliot looked back at Hickok and continued. "That fellow is out to kill you. He stated as much in the coach. At the time, he was quite furious with all of us and blurted out the truth, and I am sure he meant it."

"Oh, he meant it, all right," Mike Williams spoke up.

"Yes," agreed Connie Witherspoon. "He certainly did. A most unpleasant man, I assure you. I am sure he has a grudge of some kind against you, Mr. Hickok."

Hickok smiled at them. "There's quite a few in this town and elsewhere have a grudge against old Wild Bill. Comes with the job. Maybe this feller was just shootin' off his mouth. Talk is cheap, they say."

"We hope you're right," said Elliot, "but we felt it our responsibility to warn you of his threat."

"And I am right glad you did warn me." He turned to Connie Witherspoon. "Would you mind giving me that fellow's name again?"

"Of course. It's Jim Mulrey."

"Ah . . . yes," Hickok said softly, his face suddenly troubled. "I remember the name—and now the face as well. It was in Hays City where I last saw that unpleasant young gentleman."

At that moment a tall fellow with silver hair, and steel-rimmed spectacles pushed himself forward and, approaching Elliot Carson, introduced himself. He was Miles Kramer, the publisher of the *Abilene Chronicle*— and Elliot's new employer. Bidding good-bye to Hickok, Elliot hurried off with the publisher to get his luggage.

As Elliot left, Sue hurried to Mike's side and handed him his two pearl-handled revolvers, which had dropped from Mike's belt during his struggle with Mulrey. Mike thanked her and thrust his armament back into place.

Watching him, Hickok smiled. "Hell, young man, you don't need them weapons! Them fists of yours will do nicely, I'd say. Besides, I'm thinking of getting a town ordinance passed, banning the carrying of firearms in Abilene."

Mike, his face a sudden mask of resolve, looked up at the tall lawman. His chance had come, and he would never get a better one. Clearing his throat nervously, he said, "Mr. Hickok, I came here to Abilene to join your police force—to work with you for law and order."

Hickok smiled and then slapped Mike heartily on his shoulder. "Well, I'm full up for now, young man. But if I run into any trouble, I'll look you up. What do people call you?"

"Mike Williams. I mean it, Mr. Hickok. If you need any more deputies, I'm willing."

"You know how to use them two cannons, do you?"

"Yes, I do. I been practicing with them since last summer."

Again Hickok smiled, but it was a pleased smile, and there was no way Mike Williams could possibly take offense. "That's good to know, Mike. And I'm thinking any man who can use his fists like that would make a fine partner in a scrape. So keep your nose clean, and maybe I'll look you up."

Bidding good-bye to Mike then, Hickok turned and pushed his way through the few remaining spectators. As he gained the wooden sidewalk, he heard a woman calling him by name.

He halted and turned to see one of the women passengers hurrying toward him. She was older than Hickok by perhaps five years, and she appeared vaguely familiar. From the expression on her face, Wild Bill got the impression that they must have met somewhere before.

Touching the brim of his hat to her, he smiled. "Yes, ma'am, what can I do for you?"

"I need help, James. Would you be willing to help an old acquaintance?"

Hickok frowned. "Of course, ma'am, but I . . . Wait a durn minute! Aren't you with that circus, the one that was here this summer?"

"Yes, James. I'm Agnes Thatcher. You knew my husband, Bill." She smiled. "Remember that impromptu exhibition you gave for our circus in Denver two years back?"

"*Of course!*" Hickok exploded after a moment's hesitation. "And how is Bill?"

"Dead these past six months, I'm afraid," Agnes said. "But he left me enough money to travel, and I thought I would like to spend some time in Abilene. It is the most famous trail town in the country—and you must be the most famous town marshal."

The tall lawman shook his head ruefully. "Them crazy New York papers. They just don't know what the truth of it is. And them reporters sure can spread whoppers. What's a man to do?"

She smiled patiently. "Well, for the moment, you could help me with my bags and direct me to the Drovers' Cottage."

"I'd be delighted," Hickok said, turning back with her to search out her luggage amidst the growing pile beside the stagecoach.

Elliot Carson had separated his luggage and was about to depart with Kramer when he saw Connie Witherspoon struggling with her bags. Excusing himself, he left the publisher and hurried over to Connie's side.

She did have a great deal to carry: two trunks, a valise, and a rather worn carpetbag.

"Can I help, Miss Witherspoon?"

Startled, Connie looked up at Elliot. "Why no, Mr. Carson. I am expecting someone. I'll be all right, thank you."

There was in her voice not the slightest trace of warmth. Though they had covered many weary miles together, nothing in her manner indicated any interest in continuing their relationship beyond the confines of that crowded stagecoach.

Elliot looked at the amount and heft of her luggage in some confusion. "Are you sure, Miss Witherspoon? I would be glad to help, I assure you."

"And I assure you," said Connie, her voice firm, her chin solid with resolve, "that I do not need your assistance. I am expecting someone."

Touching the brim of his hat in good-bye, Elliot backed quickly away, then turned around to rejoin Miles Kramer.

On Kramer's face was an ironic smile. "Don't appear to me you made much of an impression on *that* young lady," he commented, "though I can't say as I blame you for your interest in her."

"She got on at Omaha, and I have been doing all that I could ever since," Elliot admitted with a smile. "But I do not intend to let her current attitude discourage me. I like a challenge, Mr. Kramer."

The publisher laughed. "Call me Miles," he said. "And if it is challenge you want, you've come to the right place. Being managing editor of the *Abilene Chronicle* may prove enough of a challenge for now. As soon as we get you settled, we'll go to dinner and I'll fill you in."

"That suits me fine," said Elliot, as the two men, each lugging heavy baggage, hurried off.

*   *   *

Mike Williams moved forward until he was beside Sue Ann Mobley, who was struggling with a carpetbag and trunk. All Mike had to carry was a light canvas valise.

"Let me help, Sue Ann."

She turned quickly to face him, a smile brightening her cute, perky face. "Oh, thank you!" she said. "I never realized these bags were so heavy. It's like they got heavier with each mile to Abilene."

Mike laughed. "All that dust, maybe."

After a moment of sizing up the problem, Mike suggested they leave the heavier baggage at the express office, and he would return for it later, when she had found a place to stay. Sue Ann readily agreed, and the two soon set out to look for lodgings.

The last of the passengers, Major Horace Farber, grasped his sole piece of luggage, a battered leather valise, and set off down Texas Street. He would see to his lodging later. At the moment he was as dry as a preacher's sermon, his flask having been emptied by that last nip outside Abilene.

The hustling, wide-open town impressed him. From the look of it, Abilene was all it was cracked up to be. Cowboys hot off the Chisholm Trail from Texas were walking boldly four abreast down the streets sporting duds newly purchased and wearing six-shooters on their hips and wild looks in their eyes. The major did not find it difficult to imagine money burning holes in their fresh Levi's.

All these young fellows loved to gamble—the major knew that for a fact. Taking a deep breath, he reflected that almost all of his remaining fortune had gone to purchase the ticket for the stagecoach to get here, but it had been a wise investment. Without a doubt, Abilene was the place for a man with luck to turn his fortune around. A single roll of dice . . . the flip of a card . . . it would not take more than that, and a rosy future would once more beckon to him.

But first that drink. Ahead of him, across from the jail, he spied an outrageous sign depicting an enormous red bull, its most important attribute startlingly visible and apparently in fine working order. The Bull's Head saloon was only one of seven or more bars where a man could drink, gamble, and find female companionship for the night. Smiling broadly, the major directed his steps toward the Bull's Head.

No longer on Texas Street, but on a narrow side street two blocks over, Sue Ann and Mike found the rooming house they had been directed to by a woman they had stopped in some desperation on the street a moment before. The place did not look very promising. Its front porch sagged dangerously, and one shattered downstairs window had been clumsily boarded up. But this was the third place they had tried, and each landlady had looked with cold, reproving eyes on Sue Ann the moment she told them she was alone and unattached. There was little doubt why: Girls alone in Abilene usually found a home eventually—but not in the respectable parts of town.

"You let me handle this," Mike told Sue Ann, as he knocked on the door. "Don't say a word."

A tired, washed-out woman in her late thirties answered his knock. "Yes?" she inquired almost furtively.

"Ma'am," Mike said, "my sister and I just arrived in Abilene. We'll soon be opening a restaurant in town, and we were told you have rooms to let."

"For both of you?"

"I'll be staying elsewhere with my business partner," Mike lied grandly, "but I'd like a respectable room for my sister, Sue Ann."

The landlady pulled the door open wider. "Well now," she said, "you're in luck, miss. I just happen to have a room on the second floor. I'm Ma Kitchin. Now you just follow me."

The room she showed them was dim, fetid, and barely large enough for the bed. Into one corner was crowded a mean, battered chest of drawers, and no mirror hung above it. An oil lamp sat on the floor by the bed. Blocking the single narrow window was the commode, with a bowl and a pitcher on top of it. But the room was clean enough.

Ma Kitchin had to get out of the room in order for them to be able to fit in and inspect it. Sue Ann was obviously dismayed by the cramped nature of the accommodations, but stifling a shudder, she looked wearily up at Mike and nodded unhappily.

"You're sure?" Mike asked.

With Ma Kitchin standing close by, outside the door, Sue Ann told him softly, "I guess this will just have to do."

When Mike, stepping outside the door, told Ma Kitchin his sister approved of the room, the older woman nodded briskly. "I keep my rooms clean. They ain't nothing fancy, but a body can sleep here and know he ain't a goin' to be waked up in the middle of the night and find a horse and rider in bed with him."

Moving out of the room behind Mike, Sue Ann asked, "How much is the room, ma'am?"

"One dollar a night, and that'll be a week in advance."

Sue Ann gasped and looked with sudden consternation at Mike. He simply nodded.

"That's reasonable," he managed, reaching for his wallet, "if, as you say, the place is clean. What meals come with that?"

"Breakfast, but I serve only once, and that's at seven sharp."

Sue Ann nodded meekly as Mike handed Ma Kitchin the seven dollars and told the landlady they would return with more of his sister's luggage. Folding the money swiftly, Ma Kitchin nodded grimly, tucked the bills into her bosom, turned on her heel, and led the way back down the stairs.

Outside on the street, Sue Ann looked with some concern at Mike. "I don't know how I would've managed without you, Mike. But you shouldn't have taken it upon yourself to pay for my lodgings. Her prices are simply outrageous. I am sure I could have found a cheaper place elsewhere."

"I'm not. This town is full up with free-spending cowboys. The lodging houses are just charging what the traffic will bear."

"Well, I thank you, Mike. As soon as I get a job, I'll pay you back. I promise."

He smiled. "We'll talk about that later. Now let's go get your bags. I'll bet you can't wait to sleep in a bed at last—one that isn't rocking all the time."

Sue Ann laughed in agreement.

As they hurried off back to the express office, Mike tried not to think of the fact that in handing Ma Kitchin seven dollars, he had left himself with less than five of his own to use for lodging. He comforted himself with the realization that his generous gesture was not lost on Sue Ann.

He liked Sue Ann. He liked her a great deal, and he wanted to see more of her—much more—in the weeks to follow.

As Hickok put Agnes Thatcher's bags down before the front desk of the Drovers' Cottage and waited for the desk clerk to finish with another party, Agnes looked around her in awe at the wide, thickly carpeted lobby.

"My, this place is certainly more elegant than our circus wagons," she remarked.

Hickok smiled and nodded.

"Does it have a good restaurant?"

"The best around."

"Then you must allow me to repay you for your kindness, James. Have dinner here with me tonight."

Hickok looked down at Agnes and smiled. "Now, Agnes, you know you don't have to pay me for helping you with your luggage."

She blushed. "I know that, but please allow me to use it as an excuse. I'd like very much for you to join me tonight for dinner. I'd like to hear all about your travels since you left Denver."

"On one condition."

"Name it."

"I'll not stand for you paying. In memory of a fine gentleman, your husband Bill, allow me to escort you."

"In that case, I accept your condition. But tell me, James . . . is that the only reason—the memory of my husband?"

Hickok knew precisely what his response was supposed to be, and he was quite adept at playing the game. But for some reason, he did not want to play that kind of game with this woman. She was older than he but not at all unpleasant to look upon, and there was a disarming honesty about her that had appealed to him from the beginning. In thinking back on their earlier encounter while she was Bill Thatcher's wife, he remembered feeling the same appreciation of her directness that he felt now. But it was more than that—he liked style, and this woman had it.

"My, it's taking a long time for you to answer," Agnes remarked mischievously. "You don't really have to answer. Women who ask such questions deserve the answers they get."

"I was going to say," Hickok replied with a smile, "that only time will provide better reasons for bringing us together, Agnes. For now, let me just say that it will be a pleasure for me to escort you to dinner this evening."

The gallantry of that reply pleased Agnes, and she smiled. "Shall we meet here in the lobby at eight?"

"I shall call for you then." Hickok bowed.

Agnes's smile was so radiant that in one stroke it seemed to have erased from her countenance all the dust and fatigue of her long journey, and she said, "I promise I won't keep you waiting."

When the desk clerk approached them, Agnes told him what she wanted, and as soon as Wild Bill was sure that Agnes would settle in without difficulty, he touched the brim of his hat to her and left the Drovers' Cottage. A few influential townsmen nodded or called to him by name as he swept past them on his way across the broad veranda, then strode down the steps and headed for the Alamo, a handsome oasis of drink and excitement, and the marshal's favorite saloon.

As he walked along the crowded wooden sidewalk—a full head taller than some he passed—Hickok allowed himself finally to turn his attention to that weasel of a man young Williams had been pummeling—Jim Mulrey. Ignoring the cowboys, cattle buyers, merchants, and townspeople—and the children that tore past him through the crowd with voices like scalded cats—he went over in his mind the death of Jim Mulrey's brother.

Bill Mulrey had been shooting up a saloon, and when Hickok—the Hays City sheriff at the time—arrived on the scene, Mulrey spun on him, both guns drawn. Throwing Mulrey off guard by glancing past him and pleading, "Don't shoot him, boys," Hickok drew his own revolver and killed Mulrey on the spot.

At the funeral, Hickok had glimpsed Bill Mulrey's younger brother, Jim. He could not have been twenty at the time. The little man had seemed cruelly ravaged by his older brother's death, and throughout the burial service, he had glared at Hickok with red-rimmed, hate-filled eyes. That was the last time Hickok had seen the young Mulrey until this day. . . .

"Hold it right there, Marshal!"

Hickok pulled up. A tall, lean Texas cowboy and two other drovers were standing on the sidewalk, blocking his path, their eyes trained on him like gunbarrels. It was the tall one's voice that had cut so rudely into the marshal's thoughts.

Hickok smiled coolly at the man. "What can I do for you, Tex?"

Townsmen scattered. There was suddenly no one behind either Hickok or the three Texans, and Hickok was aware of other townsmen hurrying swiftly across the street to watch the action from a safe distance.

"I got a trail herd outside of town waiting its turn in the yards," said the Texan—apparently the trail boss, Wild Bill was thinking. "And I got some young men out there been eatin' bad food, sleepin' in wet clothes, goin' without women, and now they're ready to cut the wolf loose. But we heard 'bout you down in El Paso, mister. You like to pick on southern boys, we heard. So I just come in here to tell you this here outfit won't take no horseshit from a Yankee town marshal."

"It will take what it has to, Tex. We just rebuilt that jail around the corner over there, and if any of your cowboys shoot up this town or get out of hand, they'll end up inside that lockup until it comes time for their long ride back to Texas. And I think you should know I treat Texans and Yankees just the same."

"That ain't what we heard."

30

"Hell, Tex," Hickok said softly, "what makes you think I give a damn what you heard?"

The studied insolence in that reply struck the Texan like a slap in the face. Before he could come up with a rejoinder, Hickok started on his way again and brushed angrily past him, knocking the man and his two drovers off the high wooden sidewalk.

Furious, the trail boss went for his gun. A woman across the street screamed, a high, keening cry that cut through the tension like a knife. Wild Bill, his two Colt .44s cocked and ready, spun completely around as Mike Williams darted from the crowd, both his guns drawn as well.

The three Texans froze.

"That's it. Hold it right there," Hickok said.

"Do as he says," Mike added, steadying his two guns on the trail boss. Sheepishly, the Texan allowed his six-gun to drop back into its holster; there was no sense in risking fire from both sides. His two comrades did the same.

An audible sigh of relief swept over the crowd, and from far back, a distant voice called, "Attaway, Bill!" But that was the only sound that came from the waiting townspeople as Hickok surveyed the three Texans with an icy contempt.

"I don't take kindly to Texans—or Yankees—that draw on me," Hickok told the trail boss. "Your drovers are welcome in Abilene—under the conditions I outlined a moment before—but if any of you three return, you should know you will be most unwelcome. I suggest you remain on your best behavior during your stay—your last stay—in this town." Then Wild Bill smiled coldly at the Texan and took a step toward him. "And don't you ever draw on me again, you sonofabitch, or you'll return to Texas in a pine box. You hear that?"

The trail boss nodded sullenly, then turned and

stalked off, his two companions with him. Hickok watched them go, feeling the tension easing slowly out of him.

The traffic on the sidewalks commenced again, everyone giving Hickok and Mike a wide berth. There were grins on a few faces but frowns on many others. Bloodshed had been avoided only by an eyelash, and few of those who were betting on the future of Abilene wanted this kind of trouble.

Turning to Mike, Hickok stuck out his hand. "Thanks, young man. You still looking for a job?"

Mike nodded eagerly. "I sure could use one!"

"How'd you happen to be on top of them three that fast?"

"I recognized that trail boss. Our stage got held up by his trail herd outside Abilene. I was surprised to see him here this soon."

"Tex must have ridden in ahead of the herd. Just couldn't wait for a run-in, it seems." Hickok shook his head, then peered down at Mike with obvious concern. "You realize you might have to contend with that fellow when he returns with his drovers and gets all liquored up?"

Mike nodded grimly. "I suppose that could happen . . . but that don't bother me."

Hickok studied the young man's face for an instant longer, searching perhaps for some sign that Mike was less than he appeared. Then, evidently satisfied that he had measured the young man correctly, the marshal clapped him on the back.

"Join me for a drink in the Alamo," he said. "I figure I owe you one."

Mike accepted readily, and the two moved on.

Looking down from the window of his second-story hotel room, Jim Mulrey breathed a sigh of relief. For a moment there, he had been afraid that one of those Texans was going to cheat him out of his due.

He turned away from the window and slumped down on his bed. His head throbbed, and he had given up any thought of eating until his torn mouth healed some. Besides, with his face looking the way it did now, he had no desire to be seen in public.

He blamed no one but himself. He should have kept under better control in that stage . . . and he should have kept his big mouth shut. Still, that Sue Ann really interested him. He knew the type: a run-away for sure, heading for the bright lights. There was no doubt in his mind where she would end up in this town, and when she did, he would go looking for her. He'd strip all her fancy airs from her then, make her realize—and admit to him—that for all her fine pretenses, she was no better than he.

But first he had to get his face into shape. He had plenty of time, he reminded himself. Best thing would be for him to cause no trouble at all for a while, just become a part of the town and lull Hickok into thinking he was all bluff. No reason he couldn't wait, after all. He had robbed and killed an Omaha storekeeper before setting out for Abilene, so he had plenty of money, and he knew he would have no trouble evening things with Hickok—and that punk Williams.

He leaned back on the bed and crossed his arms under his head, letting himself savor that coming triumph. He'd be famous, sure enough. . . . He'd be the man who killed Wild Bill Hickok!

Chapter 3

Connie Witherspoon followed her cousin, Annabelle Jenson, through the hall to a door. Opening it, Annabelle stepped aside, her face still pinched with resentment. The woman had not smiled once since meeting Connie at the express office.

"Your room is in here," Annabelle told her. "It is small, but it will do nicely, I am sure."

Stepping past Annabelle, Connie bent her head to enter the room, squeezed past the foot of the bed, and found herself blocked by the commode. The dresser was in the corner beyond it. With some difficulty, Connie managed to lean past the commode and place her carpetbag upon the top of the dresser. There was no window—the room was in the center of the house under the staircase. Connie would be sleeping with the stairwell inches from her head.

"Yes, this is fine, Annabelle," Connie said dutifully. "I am sure I will be very happy in here."

This response seemed to mollify Annabelle. Her long, narrow face softened somewhat. "Would you like a cup of coffee?"

"That would be fine, thank you. But first, I'd like to . . ."

"Of course. It's out back. You may use the kitchen door."

A few moments later, Connie reentered the kitchen and found Annabelle sitting at the kitchen table, upon which were set two cups of black coffee. Connie used the pump in the sink to fill a small basin and, with a thick bar of soap, washed her hands thoroughly. She sat down to sip at her coffee, which was scalding. No milk or cream was on the table.

Putting the cup down somewhat hastily, Connie let it warm her hands. "Can you tell me about the shop now?" she asked Annabelle. "I'm eager to get busy. You have no idea how grateful I am for this chance to work."

"I can imagine," said Annabelle. "I just hope *you* can imagine how surprised I was to receive your letter. As you can see, I have very little room here, and what room I do have, I must rent out to boarders. Everything is so expensive here in Abilene. And the dress shop is already fully staffed. Fortunately, the shop is doing reasonably well, so I suppose we can carry you for a while, until you begin to earn your pay." She looked sharply at Connie. "You do sew?"

"Of course."

"I mean how well do you sew? And how fast? This is a business, you must realize, not a ladies' sewing circle. I charge top dollar for my dresses, and my customers—what few there are—demand the very finest workmanship."

"I assure you, I can sew as well and as quickly as you may wish. But you must realize—I have just completed a tedious and most difficult journey. Boston is a long, long way from this cattle town."

"It was a journey you chose to make. It was, after all, you who wrote me."

Connie smiled thinly. "Yes, I am guilty as charged.

It is just that no one ever knows what something is really like until one has experienced it. Now I know about long journeys—and how far Kansas is from Boston."

"I should have thought that everyone knew experience is the only teacher."

"It may not be the only teacher, but it surely is the best."

"Yes . . . for you, at least," Annabelle said, her eyes like needles as she lifted her cup to her mouth.

Connie started to respond, then caught herself, alarmed. The two of them had met less than an hour ago, and already they were picking at each other like chickens in a barnyard. Living in this house with this woman and working six days a week under her cold scrutiny was going to be difficult—far more difficult than she could ever have imagined.

When Annabelle finished her coffee, she got to her feet. "I must get back to the shop," she told Connie. "I had hoped you might be able to start work today, but I see that you'll want to get settled in first. And there are still your trunks and that valise to be brought over. I must warn you, however, that it is extremely unwise for you to go out unescorted. At least, not until it is abundantly clear to everyone that you are a decent woman—not one of those trollops from across the tracks."

"Then how do you propose I get my things? I was planning to go back to the express office this afternoon and hire a boy to bring them for me."

"Alone?"

"Unless you would care to accompany me."

"I told you I must get back to the shop."

"Then I have no choice."

"You could wait."

Connie looked down at her coffee, then drank it, though it was as acrid in taste as her cousin was in temperament. She would go for her things as soon as Annabelle left, despite the warning. No—*because of it*.

Looking down at Connie with pursed lips, Annabelle said, "It is my custom to serve supper at six. However, I begin preparing the meal at five and will expect you to do what you can to help. I think that's only fair."

Connie nodded. "Only fair," she repeated.

After Annabelle left, Connie leaned her head back against the wooden chair and let her legs stretch out under the table as far as they would go. After the constant rolling and pitching of the stage, just to be able to sit with her body still had become one of life's greatest luxuries. The only other luxury to come close was the absence of Annabelle.

She got up and poured herself another cup of coffee, hunted fruitlessly for cream or milk, then sipped the bitter liquid slowly, considering her options. She really had none; she was here in Abilene at her cousin Annabelle's mercy, and that was simply all there was to it.

Of course, she could get married again—flee headlong into the strong arms of some man who would take her away from Annabelle and put her in his kitchen . . . and his bedroom. Connie shook her head with sudden, bitter determination. *No*, she would keep to her fine oversized closet and stick it out with Annabelle and her dress shop . . . for now.

She got up, washed her cup in the sink, set it upside down on the counter, then found her hat, adjusted it on her head, and walked from the small house. The street was so narrow that only a single horse cart could pass at a time. The area was filthy, and in the close, dusty air, the stench of horse manure hung almost as heavily as the swarm of horseflies.

Holding her skirts up past her ankles, Connie hurried down the street until she reached a broader avenue, crossed that, and then continued on until she reached the broadest avenue in Abilene: Texas Street. The express office was just about three blocks away.

She found herself part of a rude throng. Cowboys and others equally rough looking swept past her, jostling her wordlessly, not even attempting to excuse themselves. The shaky wooden sidewalk trembled and rang to the harsh tramp of their boots and the jingle of their spurs, and from all around her came the hammering and sawing of wood as carpenters busied themselves putting up new buildings.

Texas Street—Abilene's main thoroughfare—not only had the most prosperous businesses but also was lined with the fanciest buildings. One of these was the Drovers' Cottage, the grandest hotel in town. Towering three stories high, it was painted in bright yellow with green trim. Connie noticed the fashionable venetian blinds in its windows—soon to become its trademark. Behind the Cottage was a stable with room for a hundred horses and fifty carriages. The food in the dining room was reputed to be as good as that of the poshest eastern restaurant, and its lounges were praised as places where businessmen could think and talk in genteel quiet. On its broad veranda, too, drovers could relax, make deals, or just sit and watch the trains go by.

Around the corner from the Drovers' Cottage were the stockyards, where every day of the summer the cattle pawed the ground and cracked their horns together as they waited their turn to be weighed, sent up the ramp, and loaded onto the trains that would take them to stockyards in St. Louis and Chicago. Although she was walking away from that end of town, Connie could still hear the continual bawling of the cattle.

All this change of scene, the unfamiliar sights and sounds—not to mention the smells—only served to depress Connie even further. She was beginning to think she would never see a well-shaved face again—or brush past a man that did not smell like a horse. And the flies! They were big enough and persistent enough to carry her off, she thought grimly as she swiped at them with futility.

Indeed, so intent was she on getting rid of one particularly pesky fly that she momentarily lost her balance. When she tried to right herself, someone struck her from behind with just enough force to nudge her off the crowded sidewalk—and she found herself in the street alongside it. With a shrug she continued on, perfectly willing to keep to the street and off that swarming walkway.

Lost in her thoughts, Connie did not at first notice the sharp clatter of hooves as four horsemen wheeled out of an alley leading from the loading pens and started to gallop abreast down Texas Street. A few buggies and one freighter had to swerve suddenly to avoid the hard-galloping riders. Abruptly, in an excess of high spirits, the cowboys took out their six-guns and punctured the sky with hot lead.

The thunderous detonations almost caused Connie to jump out of her skin. In a panic, she spun around. Shading her eyes, she saw one of the riders cut his horse sharply and spur straight for her. Reining up so suddenly that his horse reared—its forelegs pawing the air dangerously close to Connie's head—the cowboy swept off his sombrero and grinned down at her. He was a mere stripling, Connie saw at once, no more than eighteen or nineteen, if he was that.

"Howdy, ma'am!" the Texan shouted gleefully, fully aware that everyone on the street was now watching. "Are y'all out here to welcome me to Abilene City?"

"Not on your life!" retorted Connie, as she started quickly on down the street away from the rider.

But the Texan would not be dismissed this lightly. Leaping from his horse, he grabbed Connie's arm with one hand, encircled her waist with the other, and began to whirl her about in an impromptu dance. Soon his comrades were galloping around them in a circle, whooping like Comanches.

Connie tried desperately to twist out of the cowboy's grasp, but she had no luck at all, and so violently did the Texan whirl her around that she was having difficulty keeping on her feet. To her utter astonishment and dismay, the townsmen on the sidewalk—instead of rushing to her aid—stood perfectly still, and the other cowboys took off their hats and began to cheer the crazy cowpoke on!

Desperate—and furious—Connie began to scream at the top of her lungs.

Earlier, after showing Elliot to his rooming house, Miles Kramer had invited his new managing editor out to dinner at his favorite restaurant, a block down from the Drovers' Cottage. As soon as they had ordered, the publisher, in response to Elliot's queries, launched into an account of Abilene's remarkable history.

"T. C. Henry and Joe McCoy were Abilene's cofounders," Kramer began, "though I guess you might say most of the credit should go to McCoy. He was the first to come on this here town when it was not much more than a pimple on the backside of this Kansas prairie."

Elliot laughed. "How big a place was it, exactly?"

"A dozen log huts, and maybe that's giving it more credit that it deserves. But of course it was right alongside the Kansas Pacific tracks, and that's what Joe was looking for. He saw at once he had found the perfect spot for his cattle town."

"When was this?"

"The spring of '67. And by that summer, McCoy had sent T. C. Henry and another man, W. W. Sugg, south looking for cattle."

Elliot frowned slightly. "You mean he had no commitment already? He just sent those two out looking for cattle? Suppose they had found none?"

"Oh, hell. Joe knew there were trail herds on the way. What he wanted was for T. C. and Sugg to intercept them. And sure enough, two hundred miles into Indian territory, those two found the Texas trail herds they were looking for and convinced the Texans to cut east for Abilene."

Elliot frowned. "But surely Abilene couldn't have been ready that soon."

"It damn well had to be," Kramer responded, shaking his head in a mixture of wonderment and admiration. "During that first hectic summer, Joe built a set of stock pens sturdy enough to contain three thousand longhorns—and along with it a ten-ton scale capable of weighing twenty cows at a time." Kramer grinned at Elliot. "And then the fellow went right on and erected the livery stable, a barn, an office—and the Drovers' Cottage."

"You're right," responded Elliot. "Joe McCoy should get the lion's share of the credit for creating this place."

"Of course, the first herds arrived before everything was completed, but by the end of that first season, in November, McCoy and T. C. Henry had shipped out more than one thousand carloads of cattle."

"Impressive . . . very impressive," Elliot said. "To think that overnight, almost, he transformed twelve log huts into a rip-roaring trail town famous throughout the country."

As the waiter came with their drinks, Kramer nodded. "Yes, Elliot—famous. But infamous, as well, I am afraid. It is my hope, however, that you have ar-

rived at another crucial turning point in Abilene's remarkable history. Indeed, I am convinced of it."

"How so?" Elliot asked, as he sat back to sip his
drink.

"As a cattle town, Abilene is finished," Kramer
asserted boldly. "During these past three years, a steady
stream of farmers has come to Abilene, and—unlike Joe
McCoy—T. C. Henry has been quick to encourage it. I
hear tell his real-estate office has been selling ten to
fifteen farms a day. To my way of thinking, Elliot, those
farmers—not Texas longhorns—represent the real future of Abilene. This is prime farmland, after all. The
Texans and their cattle will just have to go elsewhere
and leave this town to the farmers and businessmen
who serve them. Only in this way can Abilene grow as
it should into a decent, law-abiding community."

Frowning thoughtfully, Elliot said, "But surely there
must be elements in Abilene determined to keep things
just as they are."

"You are most astute, Elliot. Indeed, Phil Coe and
Ben Thompson, gamblers and gunmen both of them,
are actively opposing any element in Abilene that would
boot the Texans out. And of course, Joe McCoy sides
with them."

"And what has been the *Chronicle*'s stand on all
this?"

"I have no doubt that the future of Abilene rests
with the farmers," Kramer replied with a smile.

Elliot nodded curtly. "I see. Tell me, what kind of
a job has Wild Bill Hickok been doing?"

"As the *Chronicle* has made clear on more than
one occasion, it regards Wild Bill's tenure as town
marshal in Abilene as an unmitigated disaster. He spends
most of his time in the Alamo playing poker or with his
ladies of the evening. And he allows these Texans to

wear their six-guns in town. He's certainly not the man
Tom Smith was."

"Tom Smith?"

"Bear River Tom Smith was our first town marshal.
He was a former New York City policeman. He did a
fine job."

"What happened to him?"

"A farmer killed him . . . with an ax."

Elliot winced. "But while he was the marshal, *he*
had been able to convince the Texans to remove their
sidearms?"

Kramer nodded. "And he never had to fire a shot.
For the most part he relied on his fists. A braver, finer
peace officer I have never met. It was a sad day for
Abilene when we buried that man."

Elliot leaned back and sipped his drink. Their meal
had not yet arrived, but already he had a great deal to
digest. What particularly astounded him was Kramer's
estimation of Wild Bill Hickok's worth. Elliot himself
had been mightily impressed by the marshal when he
waded in to stop that fight between young Mike Williams and Jim Mulrey. And in the short conversation
with Wild Bill that followed, Elliot had been impressed
by the man's appearance and impeccable manners. It
was clear he was a gentleman.

It was just as clear that Miles Kramer approached
Wild Bill Hickok from a completely different angle than
did Elliot. Elliot hated violence—the war had shown
him how vicious an instrument it could be—but Wild
Bill was dealing with men just off the trail, men looking
for trouble. This fellow Tom Smith had been a man who
could rely on his fists, perhaps, but Wild Bill had no
choice but to make use of his considerable reputation as
a gunfighter.

Of course, the ideal solution would be for Abilene

to make neither a Tom Smith nor a Wild Bill Hickok necessary.

Gunfire erupted from the street outside, and with it Elliot and Miles Kramer heard the high yip of inebriated cowboys. Both men winced but continued to drink. It was strange, Elliot realized, but after a while decent people were quite capable of putting up with almost anything. As the gunfire and shouting continued, Elliot looked around him at the other diners, who pretended not to hear a thing as they talked a little louder and continued with their meals. *Incredible,* he thought.

Then came a scream, high and terrifying. Again and again its sound pierced the air. Glancing out the window beside him, Elliot saw a crowd rushing along the sidewalk.

"Dammit!" Elliot cried, jumping to his feet. "What in hell's going on out there?"

Miles was less eager to find out. He got up, but reached out a hand to restrain Elliot. "Don't be so anxious to stick your neck out. It's probably some whore riding bare-assed down the street with a Texan. It has happened before, I assure you."

The screaming, however, continued—and this time it was punctuated with gunfire. Elliot could restrain himself no longer, and as he rushed from the restaurant, Miles Kramer trailed reluctantly after him. Once out on the sidewalk, they saw what the commotion was and halted.

Some girl—perhaps a whore as Miles had suggested—was dancing in the street with a Texan while his mounted companions fired into the air as a sort of accompaniment. Elliot was about to return to the restaurant with Miles when the girl turned and he got a good look at her face.

Connie! It was Connie Witherspoon! And she was

not dancing with pleasure. Tears of outrage and embarrassment were coursing down her cheeks!

Elliot dashed out into the street, ignoring Miles Kramer's shouted plea not to get involved. Bursting recklessly through the ring of horsemen, he grabbed the shoulder of the Texan and flung him away from Connie.

The cowboy tripped and fell backward to the ground. Then, yelling with delight, he scrambled to his feet and launched himself at Elliot. With icy calm, Elliot waited for the proper moment, then stepped inside the range of the man's flailing fists and planted a sledging blow on the point of his chin. So completely did Elliot follow through that his right shoulder was facing his opponent as the Texan took a single step back, stared glassy-eyed at Elliot, and then collapsed to the ground.

Elliot turned then to escort Connie back across the street to where Miles Kramer was waiting for them— but he never reached her. A high-pitched yell pierced the air as one circle of rope, then another, dropped over his shoulders. Before he knew what was happening, Elliot, lassoed like a bull, was spinning around as the downed Texan's comrades rode in a tight circle. And all the while, gunfire continued to puncture the air with hot lead.

Planting his feet firmly, Elliot almost yanked hard enough to unseat one of his tormentors, but a cruel tug from the other side caused him to stagger back. Suddenly, the ropes were loosened, and Elliot was allowed to sag wearily to the ground, where he pulled free of the ropes. The dazed cowpuncher Elliot had slugged climbed back up into the saddle, joined his fellows, and with them galloped off down Texas Street, the sound of their barbaric cries fading slowly as the wild men crossed the tracks and headed out of town.

Somewhat groggily, Elliot got to his feet and began

to brush himself off. As he did so, a cheer rose up from the spectators. Elliot froze and glared at them balefully. Where had they been, he wanted to know, when Connie was being mishandled by those apes on horseback?

Rushing to his side, Connie helped to brush the dust from his jacket. "Are you all right?" she asked anxiously. Her tears, now slackening, made her eyes seem to glow with concern for him.

"I'm fine," he muttered. "What about you?"

She smiled weakly. "I'm still a little bit dizzy, but otherwise I'm fine. Where on earth did you come from?"

"I was with a friend in a restaurant down the street when I heard the commotion. We were about to have dinner." A sudden thought occurred to him, and he smiled. "Won't you join us?"

"Thank you," she said, almost humbly. "That sounds very nice."

As the crowd broke up, Elliot escorted Connie back across the street to the waiting Miles Kramer.

After introductions were made, the three went inside, and Connie gave her order to a waiter, who then hurried off. Miles Kramer, looking at the young woman sitting across from him, shook his head ruefully.

"I must apologize, Miss Witherspoon. I should have been out there in the street alongside Elliot, but . . . well, so much of that sort of thing is constantly going on in Abilene that most of us tend to pay it no heed. And for the most part, it is perfectly harmless."

"Harmless? You regard baboons on horseback shooting off firearms in the middle of a busy street as *harmless*?"

"Of course not, Miss Witherspoon, but there is just so much of it going on during the cattle season that I am afraid we have allowed ourselves to become adjusted to it."

Connie took a deep breath and glanced with some

approval at Elliot. "Well, I for one am certainly glad that Mr. Carson has not been here long enough to allow himself to become adjusted to such goings-on. For my part, I was terrified—as any decent woman would be at such an abrupt and violent encounter."

Elliot reached out and took her hand. She looked at him with deep gratitude and smiled, and then she turned back to Miles Kramer.

"I must confess, Mr. Kramer, I find it hard to believe that the women of this town—the decent women, that is—are willing to put up with such shenanigans. When my cousin advised me against leaving her lodgings unescorted, I must admit I was not entirely convinced that such a precaution was truly necessary. I can see now that it most certainly was."

"I agree," said the hapless Kramer. "It is most definitely a disgrace."

Connie fixed Kramer with a steely glance. "Yes, it surely is. But tell me, Mr. Kramer, how is it that the fine, upstanding men of this community—men such as yourself—allow this to go on?"

Kramer, plainly discomfited by Connie's bold question, cleared his throat nervously and glanced at Elliot for some help, but Elliot simply leaned back in his chair and let the publisher answer, as interested as Connie in Kramer's response.

"We have a police force, run by Wild Bill, as you know," Kramer explained. "We leave it to them to curb the cowboys when they get out of hand, but as I mentioned, there is no harm in most of this tomfoolery . . . just young men off the trail letting off steam." He glanced at Elliot then. "Surely, you can understand that, Elliot. Those cowboys didn't really injure you, did they? And they were laughing all the time."

"Maybe they were laughing, Miles, but I wasn't. No man—and no woman—likes to be made to look a

47

fool in the presence of his fellow townsfolk. Like Connie, I found nothing pleasurable in that performance, and the potential for trouble—bad, ugly trouble—was lurking just below the surface."

"I agree," said Connie.

Kramer leaned back and smiled broadly—as if all this time he had been acting as the devil's advocate. "Good! Capital! It is clear to me that you see our problem here, both of you. And that is why, Elliot, the *Abilene Chronicle* must take a stand against the cattle trade. It must do all that it can to rally the businessmen in this town, to make them realize the folly of continuing to cater to the Texans and their wild and at times uncontrollable hungers and vices."

"What about the women in this town, Mr. Kramer?" Connie interjected. "Are you going to leave it only to the men? I suggest you enlist the women of Abilene in this crusade as well. It seems to me they have the most to gain by seeing the cattle trade go elsewhere."

"And how would you suggest the *Chronicle* do that?"

"By addressing the decent women directly from your pages, by appealing to them, by arousing them." Connie smiled somewhat ironically then. "I am sure they will know how to address their own menfolk in return."

"I agree with Connie," said Elliot.

Kramer looked shrewdly at Connie for a moment. "I like the way you express yourself, young lady. What did you do before you came here, if I may ask?"

"I worked in a library in Boston."

"A library?"

"Yes, the Boston Public Library. You have heard of it?"

"Indeed, I have. Soon we will have schools and churches in Abilene. And not long after, I hope, a library." He studied her for a moment, his eyes alight with mischief. "Then I take it you can read and write, Miss Witherspoon."

"Of course."

Kramer turned to Elliot. "There's your ladies' page editor, Elliot. I am sure she will do nicely."

"Ladies' page?"

"Yes, the *New York Herald* has just started one. News for and about women, primarily, but a column discussing other events of the day is included." Kramer looked at Connie. "You could address the women of Abilene from such a forum, Miss Witherspoon, could you not?"

"Yes, but . . . I have never done such a thing."

"You do not fancy yourself a reporter, is that it?"

"It's not that. I just never gave it any thought at all . . . until this minute."

"I think you would do famously," Kramer said, "but of course, if you have other plans . . ."

Connie came to a quick decision. "Why, Mr. Kramer, I think I would like very much to write for your paper. It does seem strange, I know, for a woman to be working on a newspaper, but surely it would do no harm for me to try."

"None whatsoever," the publisher stated emphatically. "Just keep your dander up, Miss Witherspoon, and remind your readers that they, too, have a stake in seeing an end to this cattle trade. Abilene is ready to join the rest of the civilized world. We want churches, schools, and . . . yes, libraries. As you say, our women readers will know how to address their menfolk on the subject." Kramer glanced at his managing editor. "What do you think, Elliot?"

For just a moment, Elliot looked uncertain. He was obviously somewhat taken aback by this sudden inclusion of Connie Witherspoon on his staff. What had been an interesting bit of speculation a moment before had suddenly become a reality.

"Are you quite sure, Connie," he asked, frowning in evident concern, "that you would not mind the grind of a newspaper? It will be hard work, you know. Deadlines, ink everywhere, a full working day . . . and you will be dealing with the public—a very rough public."

Connie understood Elliot's reluctance at once, for she had encountered this supposed concern before and knew precisely what it meant: Some workplaces were for men only. And Connie knew that at such workplaces women need not apply. To her dismay, Elliot evidently felt this way about a newspaper office.

"I am quite capable of handling the job, I am sure, Elliot," she told him, her eyes flashing. "I am not afraid of hard work—no woman that I know ever has been. Is there some other reason why you would rather I not take Mr. Kramer's kind offer?"

"Of course not," Elliot replied hastily. "I just wanted to make sure you knew what you were doing—that you didn't make a mistake. That's all."

"She'd make a mistake if she didn't take my offer, Elliot," Kramer said with a laugh. "And if she can get the decent womenfolk in this town to light a fire under those who want to continue the cattle trade, she will be worth her weight in gold." Kramer looked at Connie and smiled warmly to encourage her. "I have a hunch you'll do fine," he said. "Just keep that fire in your eye, young lady. I wouldn't want you to lose that."

"Don't worry about that, Mr. Kramer," Connie responded. "As long as Abilene is at the mercy of these rude cowboys, I won't rest easy."

"Fine!"

"I'll be in my office first thing tomorrow morning, Connie," Elliot said. "At seven o'clock. Miles and I will be looking forward to welcoming you to the *Chronicle*."

50

"Thank you," Connie said, blushing with pleasure.

Their dinners arrived, and Connie spent the meal doing what she could to carry on normal conversation, though her head spun dizzily throughout. She could hardly believe her good fortune. Not long before, she had been looking forward to a grim, even forbidding job as a seamstress in a dress shop run by a woman who obviously felt nothing but irritation at her presence. And now here she was about to become a member of the staff of the *Abilene Chronicle*! It was almost too much for her to take in all at once.

At the conclusion of the meal, Miles Kramer insisted on a champagne toast, and after filling each glass to the brim, Miles raised his own glass. "To the success of the *Chronicle* and to a prosperous and peaceful future for Abilene," he said solemnly. "And may you two help bring both about."

The three glasses clinked merrily. Connie swallowed the champagne and felt the bubbles tickling her nose. She sneezed, and the two men laughed. Looking at them somewhat giddily, Connie said, "I am not drunk, but I *am* worried. I am sure Annabelle is going to wonder whatever happened to me."

Elliot put down his glass. "Annabelle?"

"My cousin. It was her dress shop I was supposed to go to work in tomorrow morning. That's why she has given me a room in her house."

Elliot frowned. "You think there might be trouble? Surely, she will understand."

Connie shook her head solemnly. "I don't think so."

"Then I will go with you and explain. If you have to leave, I am sure we can find a suitable place for you."

"Absolutely," chimed in Miles. "My wife knows plenty of respectable rooming houses where you can find decent lodgings."

"That would be very kind of you."

"Then you will let me accompany you back to your cousin's?" asked Elliot.

Connie looked at the man, studying him boldly. She was remembering how distantly she had regarded him earlier that same day. Her resolution not to become involved with any man still was firm. But he was the one who had saved her from that insane cowboy, and now here he was offering to help her escape from Annabelle's baleful influence. Quietly, she sighed. She would simply have to do what she could to keep this man at a safe distance—and that would not be easy. There was too much about him she already liked.

"Thank you, Elliot," she told him. "I would appreciate that."

Annabelle answered the door. The moment she saw Elliot standing beside Connie, her face hardened in cold resolve.

"I see you have returned," Annabelle said coldly, ignoring Elliot.

"Annabelle," Connie replied happily, "this is Mr. Elliot Carson. He is the editor of the *Abilene Chronicle*, and I am going to work for him, starting tomorrow. Isn't that exciting?"

Annabelle looked at Elliot with some surprise, then back at Connie. "Just when did all this come about?" she demanded. "I thought you were to go to work in the dress shop tomorrow. That was our understanding, if I am not mistaken."

"But I thought you didn't really need me . . . and this is such a good job."

"Is it? Working beside men in a newspaper office? Really, Connie, I wondered what kind of unwomanly nonsense you had carried with you from Boston. Now I realize how right my intuitions were."

"Please, Annabelle. There is no need to talk like that."

"Oh, yes, there is. I think you had better remove your belongings from my house. You will not be staying here another minute." She looked at Elliot with a sudden, ugly smirk. "I will let your gentleman friend provide you with a place for the night. I am sure that is what you had planned from the very beginning."

As she spoke, she turned her back on them, disappearing into the house. Connie led Elliot to the room where she had left her carpetbag, and a moment later, with Elliot carrying it, they were descending the front steps. When they reached the sidewalk, the door slammed shut behind them, loudly.

Elliot grinned down at Connie. "That woman surely did not think well of me. I think I'm glad you are out of her house—and her clutches."

"Even if it means I am going to get ink all over myself?"

He laughed. "You must not mind me, Connie. Sometimes I do not think very clearly. I realize that there are worse things than having ink stains. Now let us see to your lodgings. I hope we can find you a room somewhat larger and more comfortable than that rathole your cousin had for you."

As Connie set off down the street with Elliot, she felt as if she were in the midst of a dream, a delightful, adventurous, topsy-turvy dream in which the most remarkable things could—and did—happen. If so, she was hoping against hope she would not have to wake up from it . . . at least, not for a while.

Chapter 4

His face still a mess from the thrashing he had taken at the hands of Mike Williams, Jim Mulrey left his room early that same evening, entered the swarm of people flowing past his hotel, and headed for the Bull's Head saloon. He was a secretive, gray creature dressed in a battered wide-brimmed hat, torn cotton shirt and dark woolen pants, and boots so scuffed and worn that near the heel of the right one, portions of his foot showed through.

Despite his earlier decision to stay in his room, Mulrey was so eager to feed his vices that he was willing to endure the stares from those he passed. At times he had to suppress a malicious desire to shove his battered body into the faces of those startled women he encountered. *Damn their fine sensibilities*, he thought angrily as he brushed on past them.

Suddenly Mulrey halted and, seething with hatred, stared down the street. For the second time that day, he was looking at the man he had come to Abilene to kill. Wild Bill was standing with Agnes Thatcher on the Drovers' Cottage veranda, and the two appeared to be chatting quietly as they looked out over the busy street. Just as they turned to follow a waiter into the hotel's restaurant, Mulrey caught their attention, and certain

54

they were still watching him, the bitter man did nothing to veil the fury surging through his veins.

Moving away from the Drovers' Cottage, Mulrey skulked along the wooden sidewalks for a few blocks, crossed the street, and entered the Bull's Head saloon. Crowding up to the bar, he ordered a bottle of whiskey, from which he quickly poured himself a drink. Then the gray man turned around and leaned back against the bar, choosing to ignore those who sidled quickly away from his soiled person.

Most of the tables were occupied with poker players, and one table against the far wall especially intrigued him. There sat a young girl who almost took his breath away. The men called her Jess. Very pretty, with reddish curls down to her bare shoulders, she was performing card tricks to entertain an eager crowd of four or five men. But the seductive gleam in her green eyes, the purr of her husky voice—not to mention the maddeningly low cut of her red dress—promised much more than card play.

Mulrey watched her greedily for a moment and then looked away with a shrug. A woman like that could have her pick of the men around her—and she would not come cheap.

He threw the whiskey down his throat, savoring its scalding surge, and poured himself another drink. Reaching into his pocket, he spun a twenty dollar gold piece on the mahogany bar, enjoying the pleasantly surprised look on the bartender's face.

Turning away from the bar again, Mulrey spotted an empty seat at one of the poker tables. He strode over and sat down at once, giving no one at the table a chance to object.

One of the players, he noticed with evil delight, was that fool who had caused him so much trouble in the coach—Major Farber. He fixed the pink-cheeked old fart with eyes as cold as he could manage and said, "You ain't objectin' to my joining this here game, are you, Major?"

"On the contrary, Mr. Mulrey," boomed Farber, smiling broadly. "You are entirely welcome—as long as you can pay your way."

The rest of the players nodded grudgingly, and the game went on.

Still crawling with the anger and frustration of that afternoon's beating, Mulrey played recklessly, paying scant attention to the hands dealt him. He bet heedlessly, foolishly. Soon, all too soon, it seemed, he had bet more than he had on hand. The gold he had brought with him from his room was gone. Embarrassed that no more chips stood in front of him, he looked around at the other players, who watched him intently—all of them, he had not the slightest doubt, secretly pleased at his discomfort.

"Major," Mulrey said boldly, "I'm going to have to ask a favor of you, though I know you haven't been acquainted with me for long. Seems I require a loan in order to continue."

For the briefest moment, the major hesitated. Then he smiled, broadly, generously. He had, after all, won the most and seemed well on his way to repairing his fortune.

"Of course," he said grandly, pushing over two tall stacks of chips. "Your IOU will be sufficient collateral, Mr. Mulrey." He took out a cigar and lit it.

Someone thrust a pencil and a small scrap of paper into Mulrey's hand. Hastily scribbling on it the amount of the loan and his signature, he thrust the IOU back across the table at the major. "Thank you," he managed.

"My pleasure, sir," the major replied.

The game continued. This time, though Mulrey tried to play more carefully, he seemed to fare even worse. Never in all his life had he experienced such a miserable run of cards. He was about to fling his hand down upon the table and storm out of the place when he heard a commotion behind him, just inside the saloon's swinging doors.

Turning, he saw two men entering. One of them, from the looks of his collar, was a reverend, and the fellow with him was a burly, red-faced farmer at least six feet tall. In the big man's hand was something that looked like a parchment or a scroll. The burly farmer stood his ground just inside the swinging doors, the reverend standing a little to one side of him.

"Where's Ben Thompson?" the farmer bellowed. "I got a petition here!"

The redheaded girl called Jess looked with sudden concern at a man sitting beside her. A heavyset fellow with unnaturally red lips, a squashed nose, and wild, piglike eyes, he wore a black Stetson and a black, buttonless vest. Around his thick, powerful neck was a loosely tied red and white polka-dotted bandanna. "What the hell do you want, Taylor?" this fellow demanded of the farmer.

"You heard me, Coe! I want to see Ben Thompson. I got something for him!"

"He's upstairs, Taylor," the thick-necked man named Coe said, getting to his feet and stepping around to the front of the table. Mulrey noticed that the red-haired Jess was hastily gathering up her playing cards.

"Then get him," demanded Taylor, shaking the petition toward the stairway.

"You telling me what to do, Joe Taylor?" Coe responded in a threatening tone.

"I'm telling you we got a petition here to present to the owner of the Bull's Head saloon."

"I used to be part owner," Coe reminded him. "You can talk to me."

"No, I can't, Phil. Ben Thompson bought you out, so it's Ben Thompson I want."

"All right, dammit!" cried a voice from the top of the stairway. "What the hell is this all about, Taylor?"

All eyes turned toward Ben Thompson as he descended the stairs. The saloon owner was sporting a white shirt with a string tie, and his dark, neatly pressed pants were held up by broad, bright red suspenders. Tipped back on the top of his head was a derby hat. The stump of an unlit cigar protruded from the corner of his mouth. When he caught sight of the preacher standing beside Joe Taylor, his dark, Irish eyes gleamed sinisterly.

"I got a petition for you, Ben," Joe Taylor announced, "and it is signed by over five hundred citizens of Abilene. We want you to pull down that sign outside. It's pretty damn offensive, and you know why."

Ben Thompson leaned back and roared, "Sure, I know why, but it sure as hell catches the eye, don't it?"

"Ben, that's not the point. We want it taken down."

The preacher cleared his throat nervously. "It is an offense to all who pass this foul den," the man said, his voice firm, but surprisingly small. "A stench in the nostrils of decent men and women."

"Shut up, Swallow!" snapped Phil Coe, taking a short step toward the reverend. "Taylor's a patron on occasion—he's got that going for him. But you . . . you just keep that mealymouth of yours shut, or I'll throw you out of here myself."

"You gonna read this here petition?" Joe Taylor demanded, holding it out to Ben Thompson.

"Why sure. Let me see that," Ben said, striding up to Taylor and taking the petition from him.

After Ben Thompson read it over, he tipped his gray hat comically forward, then stood back and read the statement aloud to the patrons of the crowded saloon. When he began to read the names that had been scrawled under the statement, derisive hoots followed each name. Furious, Joe Taylor tried to take back the paper, but Coe was too fast for him, snatching the petition from Thompson and tearing it in half. Then, tearing it a second time, Coe flung the pieces in Joe Taylor's reddening face. Quickly, before Taylor could recover from shock and react, Coe spun him around and booted him out through the swinging doors. A second later, Coe turned on the reverend, who only just managed to escape the clutches of his angry attacker by turning and scrambling hastily out of the saloon.

"Drinks on the house!" Phil Coe cried. "And every one of you sots drink to the long life of that beautiful bull out there and his magnificent apparatus!"

With a cheering howl of gratitude, the saloon's patrons crowded the bar for their free drink.

"Hey, now, Phil," Ben Thompson protested, "this here ain't your saloon anymore. I'll decide when to give away drinks."

"Aw, hell, Ben," Coe grinned meanly, "you can afford it!" He glanced back down at the girl he had been sitting alongside and winked. "Ain't that right, Jess?"

"Sure is, Phil," she said. "And while you're up, bring me a nightcap."

Coe bent over toward Jess and said in a husky whisper, "Maybe you'd consent to have that drink with me in my room—"

"Just get me the drink," she snapped, pushing Coe away, but then, as if to appease him, she flashed him a dazzling smile.

Coe straightened up and grinned down at the redhead. "The usual?"

"The usual," she replied.

Watching Coe brutally push his way through the crowd at the bar, Ben Thompson slumped down into a chair beside Jess. "A petition!" he exclaimed, shaking his head in some exasperation. "What's Joe Taylor and Reverend Justin Swallow going to think of next?"

"Maybe you better change that sign, Ben," Jess responded.

"Not on your life! It's a matter of pride now. No pack of bluenosed bastards is going to tell me how I can advertise my business!"

With a shrug, Jess began shuffling her cards. "Have it your way, but if there is one thing I've learned, it's that one way or another, the bluenoses usually win."

Almost as if to prove her point, Joe Taylor reappeared in the doorway, this time with two other townsmen, and all three of them were carrying revolvers.

"Damn!" cried Thompson, as he pushed back his chair and sank to his knees, pulling Jess down onto the floor beside him.

A warning shout alerted Coe at the bar. Turning, he flung a beer glass across the room toward Taylor. Then he and a big Texan beside him clawed their six-guns from their holsters and started blasting.

As everyone dove for cover, a wild fusillade devastated the saloon. A mirror behind the bar was suddenly transformed into a web of cracks, and then it collapsed. As a patron ducked away frantically, a chandelier came crashing down, and behind the bar, bottles and glasses exploded. One of the men who had entered with Taylor turned and plunged back out through the flapping doors. A moment later the second fellow, on his hands and knees, began to crawl out of the place, leaving only Joe Taylor crouched behind an overturned table to trade shots with Coe and the Texan. Down on the floor, his head nudging a cuspidor, Jim Mulrey winced, his ears ringing, as a bullet struck the stinking spittoon and whined off like an angry hornet.

"Where in hell's name is that damned Hickok?" cried Thompson.

Mulrey looked over and saw the owner crouched on the floor beside the redhead.

"I know where he is!" shouted Mulrey.

"Where, dammit?" Thompson demanded.

"He's entertaining a lady friend at the Drovers' Cottage. In the restaurant. I saw them go inside together."

"He's *what*?" Jess cried at Mulrey's words, and then beginning to rise, she said, "Why that no good—"

"Jess! For God's sake get down. Are you crazy?" Ben Thompson pulled the redhead out of the line of fire and then thundered as a slug whizzed over him, "Someone get Hickok!"

A small fellow who was crouched near the entrance flung himself to his feet and dove from the saloon. Mulrey heard his feet pounding on the wooden sidewalk as he ran off to get Wild Bill.

The restaurant of the Drovers' Cottage was nearly empty as Agnes and Wild Bill sipped the last of their coffee. Wild Bill was just winding up an account of his adventures since leaving Denver. With the exception of his meeting with Buffalo Bill, his career as a law officer had not made for a very pretty tale.

Agnes shook her head in sympathy. "Now I understand," she said.

"Understand what?" Hickok asked, raising his glass.

"When we first entered the restaurant, you refused a table that would have left your back unprotected. I understand now why you sit with your back to the wall and in clear sight of the patrons. Is this what being a famous gunfighter means?"

61

Hickok shrugged. "It is not what I want, but I find I must live with it best I can, so I try not to take too many chances, that's all. It never hurts to be careful."

Agnes shuddered. "Sounds frightening."

"At times, it is," Hickok admitted.

"Did you see Mulrey earlier, when we entered the restaurant? That look he gave us made me shudder."

"I saw him," Hickok said glumly.

"Do you have any idea why that awful man would want to kill you?"

"I do. I was forced to kill his brother two years ago in Hays City. The man gave me no choice. Of course, all Jim Mulrey cares about is that his brother is dead, and I'm the one who pulled the trigger."

"So now he must kill you."

"Yes."

"How senseless."

Hickok nodded wearily. "Sometimes, Agnes, men like him spend all their time planning what they are going to do—and seldom get to it. They lack the guts to carry out their threats."

"And you think this Jim Mulrey is that type?"

Again Hickok shrugged. "I'll know soon enough, I guess."

Agnes reached across the table and took his hand. "James," she said, "my husband left me a great deal of money. Come with me, away from this town and these killers who want only the fame that would come from killing you. We could go east."

Hickok was astonished. "Do I hear you right, ma'am?" he said, trying to keep his tone jocular. "Are you proposing to me?"

"I do not want to see you die at the hands of some cheap gunman, James. And I'd like to do what I can to prevent it." She smiled apologetically. "I know I am older than you, and I am no longer as pretty as I used

to be. But I pride myself on the fact that I am, at least
. . . not unpleasant to look upon. I know how to take
care of a man, James. You would not be sorry if we
went off from this place together—I promise you that."

"Agnes, I don't ever plan to marry," Hickok said.

Agnes smiled. "I won't tell anyone we haven't made
it official if you won't."

Hickok found this conversation difficult to believe.
"Agnes, there's something I must tell you," he began
hastily.

She released his hand and smiled. "I know. There's
someone else—is that it, James?"

"Yes, Agnes. Her name is Jess Hazell. She's a real
heller—and as good a poker player as I am. We have
our scraps, Jess and me, but I'm pretty well tied up
with her right now."

"That does not concern me, James. Of course you
must already have someone. How could it be otherwise?
But I just want you to know I am here, and that I will
wait for you—no matter how long it takes."

Hickok chuckled and shook his head. "I don't know
what to say. You have a way of coming at a man so
directly."

"With someone like you, James, I could think of no
other way."

Hickok reached over and took Agnes's hand in his.
"I admire your honesty, Agnes. I am quite flattered,
too." He smiled. "And you are right, you know—you
are not unpleasant to look upon."

Agnes blushed slightly and was about to respond
when the sound of muffled shots outside the hotel
interrupted her. The gunfire did not seem to be coming
from the street. It was probably originating from inside
a building, Hickok thought—a saloon, more than likely.

Excusing himself, Hickok hastily got to his feet and
hurried through the door leading out to the veranda. As

the rattle of gunfire continued, Hickok saw someone rushing in his direction down the street.

"Gunfight in the Bull's Head!" the fellow cried. "Phil Coe and Joe Taylor! Where's Wild Bill?"

"Over here," Hickok called, jumping down from the veranda and hurrying toward the man.

"Ben Thompson sent me to get you!" the man said, panting with excitement and exhaustion. "Coe's got a Texan on his side, and the two of them are going after Joe Taylor!"

Hickok did not need to hear any more. As he left the man and trotted down the center of the street, two of his deputies—Wilt Coffee and Frank Ames—left the crowd surging along the sidewalk toward the Bull's Head and joined him. A moment later the three men, guns drawn, burst into the saloon.

The place was a shambles, but quiet. The barkeep was lighting two lamps and setting them up on the bar. Ben Thompson rushed over to the marshal.

"Upstairs!" he told Hickok. "Phil Coe and a Texan are up there after Joe Taylor! They'll kill him!"

Hickok nodded curtly and, brushing past Thompson, headed for the stairs. Both guns drawn, he turned and called back to his deputies, telling them to clear the saloon; then he continued on up the stairs. Halfway up, he caught sight of Phil Coe peering through the balustrade.

"Go on back down, Phil," Hickok told him, "and stay down!"

Coe rose, and for a moment it appeared that he was going to offer Hickok an argument.

"You heard me, Coe!" Wild Bill shouted.

Cursing under his breath, Coe stuck his six-gun back into its holster and moved down the stairs past Hickok, who then continued up. Reaching the landing at the top, Hickok bent low and started down the dimly lit hallway. Coming to a door that was slightly ajar, Wild Bill stopped and listened for even the slightest sound from within. Hearing nothing, he pushed it all the way open. It creaked slightly on its hinges.

Suddenly a heavy detonation exploded at his left, and a streak of fire lanced at him from that end of the darkened hallway. As the bullet whispered past his cheek, Hickok pivoted and fired repeatedly in the direction from which the shot had come. After his ears stopped ringing from the shots, Wild Bill heard a groan, followed by the sound of a gun thumping to the floor. Hurrying down the hallway, he came upon a lean cowboy writhing on the floor, both hands clutching his gut. The sprawled figure was swearing softly, intently, in a decidedly Texan drawl.

"Taylor!" Hickok cried out to the darkness. "You up here?"

"Right behind you, Marshal!" Taylor said, stepping through the doorway beside him.

Hickok turned to him. "Get on downstairs, Joe. And send up Wilt and Frank. This Texan's hurt bad."

"He was after me, Marshal—him and Coe! You did the right thing!"

"Never mind that, dammit! Get my deputies up here, and then send for a doctor before this poor sonofabitch bleeds to death!"

Taylor turned and bolted down the hallway. Hickok looked unhappily down at the man he had just shot. He didn't look so good, and that did not make Hickok feel any better. But why had the stupid sonofabitch fired on him like that?

Hickok went inside the room where Joe Taylor had taken refuge, found a lamp, and lit it. Bringing it out, he set it down beside the wounded Texan. As soon as the light struck his contorted face, Hickok knew the answer to his question: This Texan was one of the two that had joined the trail boss in threatening Hickok earlier. Aware it was the marshal coming up that hallway, the Texan had tried to even the day's score.

The two deputies thumped up the stairs and hurried down the hallway to the marshal's side. "Keep an eye on him until the doc gets here," Hickok told them. "I'm going downstairs to have a talk with Ben Thompson. I'd like to find out what in hell this is all about."

About ten minutes later, under the doctor's supervision, four Texans carried their wounded comrade down the stairs. Wilt and Frank were escorting them, guns drawn. Word of the shooting had swept Abilene, and outside the saloon a lot of angry Texans were milling around, looking for an excuse to cause still more trouble.

As soon as the wounded drover had been carried from the saloon, Jess Hazell stepped out of Ben Thompson's office, Phil Coe at her side. She walked up to Hickok, her eyes smoldering angrily.

"Hello, Bill."

"Hello, Jess."

"I see that fellow we sent after you found you all right."

"He found me."

Jess smiled coldly. "The word was you were entertaining a new lady friend in the Drovers' Cottage restaurant. That right, Bill?"

"That's where I was, all right. What the hell are you doing in here, Jess? I thought you worked for Kelly, at the Alamo."

"I cut my cards wherever I please, Bill." She smiled. "You ought to know that."

"And I take whomever I please to dinner. You ought to know that as well, Jess."

She was holding a full pack of cards in her right hand. Without warning, she flung the cards at Hickok, and they struck him on the face and shoulders. He brushed them off and, reaching out, pulled Jess toward him.

"I don't need any of that from you, Jess," he told her. "Now go on out of here and let me finish up with Ben. I'll see you later."

"Maybe you will, and maybe you won't. You'll see me if you can catch me!"

He grinned at her. "I ain't had no trouble so far."

She was about to take a swing at him, but the unyielding look in his eyes stopped her. Furious, she spun around and stalked out of the saloon, Phil Coe on her heels. Hickok watched the two of them disappear through the swinging saloon doors, then turned back wearily to Ben Thompson.

"All right, Ben. Now you know that the only way to settle this is to get rid of that sign. Either that, or paint over that bull's oversized organ. You've already got enough publicity from it—and more than likely a dead Texan in the bargain. What more do you want?"

"This is a free country, Bill. No one is going to make me change that sign. It stays just the way it is."

"Tomorrow morning, Ben. That's how long you've got." With that, Hickok turned and strode from the saloon.

A huge crowd had gathered in the street by this time, and Hickok saw Joe Taylor and Reverend Justin Swallow standing in the shadows. He beckoned Taylor over to him; the man came grudgingly.

"You started this shooting, Joe. From tomorrow on, if I catch you packing a sidearm inside the city limits, I'll clap you in jail. That's not a threat—that's a promise."

"Dammit, Bill! Those men laughed at our petition. Then they threw us out of the saloon."

"Never mind that," snapped Hickok. "There'll be

no more petitions. Tomorrow morning, bright and early, that sign is coming down—either that or it's going to suffer a drastic change. And that will be the end of it. But you remember what I said—I'll clap you in jail the next time I spot you in Abilene packing a sidearm."

Having made his point, Hickok brushed angrily past Joe Taylor, while the crowd that had been crushing in around them began to buzz excitedly—and the news of what Hickok had promised Joe Taylor spread.

Chapter 5

Bright and early the next morning a crowd began to gather in front of the Bull's Head saloon, eager for Wild Bill to begin the festivities, while inside the *Chronicle* office an exasperated Elliot Carson was trying to talk some reason into his new ladies' page editor—but Connie was not responding to his argument in the way that he had hoped.

"Yes," Connie said patiently. "Of course I see, Elliot. It was all right for the women of this town to walk past that sign all this time, but if I go out there to report on its demise, I am liable to be shocked into insensibility. Is that what you mean?"

"That is *not* what I mean—"

"Well, I am sorry, Elliot, but that is what it sounds like to me."

"Connie, will you please tell me why it is so important for you to witness such a crude affair?"

"The women of this town deserve to know what is going on in their midst."

"All of it?"

"Of course! How else can they judge the need for action?"

"But suppose there's trouble—"

"Then I shall report that, also."

"Hickok might fail, you know."

"And if he does, those who insist on keeping this town lawless will have won. Don't you think the women of Abilene should be warned of that?"

Elliot shook his head in frustration. "I can see there is no point in trying to reason with you, Miss Witherspoon, and so I suggest you allow me to remind you of one very pertinent fact. I am the managing editor."

"I am quite well aware of that."

"Good. Then I think you should return to your desk and get it in order. It is time you became acquainted with your responsibilities as editor of the ladies' page. Meanwhile, *I* will cover the event in question. Is that clear, Miss Witherspoon?"

"Oh, perfectly, Mr. Carson."

Elliot wanted to say more, something that would take the sting out of his foolish ultimatum; but one look at Connie's cold, unflinching gaze, and he knew that the best thing for him at that moment would be to leave immediately and cover the story. With a curt, unhappy nod, he hurried from the office.

Connie waited a moment or two until she was sure that Elliot was well on his way; then she gathered up her pencil and notepad and followed him out the door.

Elliot arrived at the Bull's Head just as Wild Bill—a sawed-off shotgun cradled in one arm—strode through the crowd and halted in front of the offensive sign. A few of the spectators cheered, but most just stepped back in silent awe as they took in Wild Bill's impressive appearance.

Sporting his finest livery, the marshal was wearing a neatly pressed, black swallow-tailed coat, a white broadcloth shirt with a black string tie knotted at his throat, and a fancy buttonless vest. His two pearl-handled

.44s were stuck into the broad maroon sash that held up his faun-colored trousers. About to initiate what could easily become a nasty confrontation with one of the town's most powerful businessmen, the man looked as though he were going to a wedding—or a funeral.

Following after him through the crowd came Mike Williams. In one hand Mike held a bucket of white paint; in the other, a paintbrush.

Ben Thompson, who had been waiting in the entrance to his saloon, now hurried down from the porch. Behind him came a small, squat fellow with a thin mustache and furtive eyes, who appeared exceedingly nervous and seemed anxious to keep to one side and just a little behind Thompson.

"I been waiting for you, Bill," Thompson told him. "This here sign is private property, and you cannot deface it without proper legal papers." Thompson turned to the little man. "Ain't that right, Finster?"

Finster nodded unhappily.

"Who the hell is this guy?" Hickok asked.

"He's my lawyer," Thompson said with a crooked grin.

"Since when?"

"Since you left my place last night. And he knows the law. You touch my property, and I can have you thrown in jail. Bein' marshal of Abilene don't give you no right to break the law." Again Thompson turned to his lawyer. "Ain't that right, Finster?"

"Oh, yes," the fellow replied, clearing his throat nervously. "There will have to be a hearing." He swallowed unhappily as he looked up at the glowering Hickok. "Due process, you know."

"Due process, eh?" Wild Bill echoed, a mad light leaping into his eye. Wheeling around swiftly, he nodded to Mike Williams, who then picked up his can of paint and walked over to a spot under the sign. At once

71

deputy Frank Ames emerged from the crowd, carrying a small stepladder. He placed the ladder down alongside Mike and stepped back. Dipping the brush carefully into his bucket of paint, Mike ascended the ladder and with quick, efficient strokes painted out the offensive organ.

A cheer went up from the crowd. The process was repeated on the other side of the sign. Another cheer, louder this time, went up, and Mike stepped back finally to admire his handiwork.

Someone in the crowd yelled, "Hey, Ben! Now you can call your place the Cow's Head!"

The onlookers roared at that. Furious, Thompson glared at Wild Bill, threatening, "You have not heard the last of this, Bill!" Then, nearly knocking Finster to the ground, Thompson whirled and stormed back into his saloon.

The festivities completed, the crowd broke up, and as Elliot could not help but notice, everyone was happy. Even those who might have been sorry to see the sign lose its most colorful attraction had to appreciate the way it had been handled—with style, impressive style. And not a shot had been fired.

Stepping forward, Elliot Carson smiled and shook Hickok's hand. "I thought you handled that beautifully," Elliot said. Then he glanced at Mike Williams, who also was beaming. "Mike, it looks like maybe you have a career ahead of you with a paintbrush."

"No, thank you," Mike replied, pointing to some white paint trickling down his wrist. "Once was enough."

As Mike and the other deputy hurried off, Elliot said, "I'd like to find out from you just what happened in the Bull's Head last night, Bill. I'm sure the readers of the *Chronicle* would like to know as well. Could we go somewhere for an interview? Over a drink, perhaps?"

"Pretty early in the day for that, isn't it?"

"Maybe. But there's some in Abilene who think your methods are too rough, especially after last night. I understand that Texan you shot is in serious condition, and some say he may not recover. If he doesn't, that will surely turn many of Abilene's citizens against you. Now if I am to help you, I must know your side of the story."

"But would you print it?"

"Of course I would."

Hickok regarded Elliot carefully for a moment or two, clearly sizing up the newcomer, wondering if he could trust the man. Then, with a shrug, he said, "All right. Join me for a drink at the Alamo. I'll tell you as much as I know."

A few minutes later, Hickok pushed into the Alamo ahead of Elliot and led him to a table in the back. As Elliot followed, he could not help but notice the exquisite care the marshal displayed upon entering the place and in selecting his table. Only when Hickok was finally seated with his back resting against the wall did he appear to relax. Earlier, during their walk to the Alamo, the big marshal had kept to the street, avoiding the townspeople crowding the sidewalks. It was clear to Elliot that Wild Bill Hickok lived in constant fear of assassination.

At this early hour the Alamo was almost empty. The only people visible were a swamper, a lush bent over a shot glass at the far end of the bar, and the barkeep, who was busy bringing up fresh stock from the cellar. Even the musicians had not yet arrived. As soon as Hickok and Elliot were seated, however, the barkeep brought over two glasses and a bottle of Maryland rye.

"I hope you like this stuff," Hickok said.

"It's a little early for me, but I do appreciate a good rye. Thank you."

Hickok poured for both of them, downed his shot in a single swallow, then peered intently at Elliot. "Go to it, Mr. Reporter."

"That shoot-out last night. What caused it exactly?"

"You mean you don't know about the reverend and his petition?"

"I know about the reverend's petition, but what caused the shoot-out that followed? Surely the reverend did not march into the Bull's Head with guns blazing."

"The reverend and Joe Taylor were sent packing from the place, and not very politely. So Taylor came back with two armed men. Phil Coe and that Texan took them on and seemed to be getting the better hand. I went upstairs to rescue Taylor from the Texan, and when the Texan took a shot at me, I shot back."

"You say he shot at you. Didn't you warn him you were coming? Didn't you ask him to lay down his weapon?"

"I did not. Even if I had, it's doubtful he would have."

"How can you be so sure of that?"

"Because he was one of the Texans who came at me earlier that same day, demanding that I let the men cut loose in any way they liked. He wanted me dead. If he'd been a better shot, I would have been."

"But I understand you emptied both guns into the Texan. Wasn't that going a bit too far?"

"I emptied one gun, the one in my right hand. I see you don't understand, Elliot. I was lucky that fool Texan didn't kill me with his first shot. But that kind of luck can't last forever, so I emptied my gun in the direction of his gun flash. I *am not* sorry I did it. . . . I want to live. I was too busy keeping alive to count how many times I pulled the trigger." He leaned back in his chair and regarded Elliot coolly.

The editor nodded grimly. "I guess I can understand that, Bill."

"I wonder if you can, Elliot."

"Of course I can—I have been shot at. I was in the war. A friend of mine caught a slug in his chest, and he was standing inches from me. I know the feeling when you are aware that someone out there in the darkness is firing at you, but it just seems in this case you might have been a little more cautious. This is not a battlefield in a civil war . . . this is Abilene, Kansas, a trail town, and we are at peace."

"For most of these Texans, Elliot, the war is still going on. We're Yankees to them, and their hatred of us dies hard. You can't turn off a war as easy as you blow out a lamp."

Elliot sighed. That made sense, certainly. Hickok had found that he was being used as a target, and under the circumstances, his instinctive reaction was perfectly understandable. At such a moment, a man does not count how many times he squeezes the trigger—not if he is intent on living, that is.

"Tell me about yourself, Bill," Elliot suggested. "I remember reading some years ago an interview you gave to Stanley of the *Weekly Missouri Democrat.* I found it most interesting."

Hickok poured himself another drink, then grinned slyly at Elliot. "That damn fool Stanley believed every whopper I told him. Then when I really piled it on, hoping he'd wise up, he just kept on putting everything down in that notebook of his! As a reporter, he was a gullible fool. Seems to me, most easterners will believe anything you tell them, so long as you stipulate it happened out west."

"Then you didn't kill one hundred men."

"Not that I know of."

"How many men have you killed then?"

Hickok looked at Elliot coldly. "I don't know, and I'm not counting."

"I see."

"I was in the war, too, don't forget. I rode for the Free-Staters for a while until I found I couldn't stomach their tactics."

"The irregulars?"

"That's right—and they were that."

"So what then?"

"Well, I worked as a teamster on the Santa Fe Trail and shot me a few buffalo. That's when I met up with Buffalo Bill. Then I rode for the Pony Express, and when that fizzled out, I went to work for the Overland Express station in Rock Creek, Nebraska."

"I heard about that, I believe. Isn't that where you shot McCanles?"

Reluctantly, Hickok nodded. "We both hankered after the same woman. McCanles came after me with a few of his friends. When it was over, I was on my way out of Rock Creek and McCanles and his two friends were dead. I had help, and the judge cleared all of us. It was not pleasant, and I have had to live down that slaughter every day since."

Elliot nodded grimly. "What did you do after that?"

"I signed on with the Union Army as a wagon master and scout."

"And that's where you met General George Custer?"

"I was one of his principal scouts, yes."

Elliot's head was bowed as he completed some notes. Then he looked up and continued. "There was a great deal concerning your experiences scouting for General Custer in that *Missouri Democrat* interview. How much of it was true?"

"As much of it as I could sneak in. But like I said,

Stanley wasn't interested in the truth. All he seemed to want were whoppers."

"That shoot-out with Tutt was true, though?"

"True enough," Hickok replied gloomily. He shook his head. "The man just goaded me. I gave him my watch to settle a debt, but he wanted more than that."

"Like what?"

"The reputation of being the man who killed Wild Bill." The marshal lifted his glass.

"So you killed him."

"I had no choice." Hickok tossed his head back as he downed his drink. Then he set the empty glass on the table and explained, "We met in the square and walked toward each other. About seventy-five yards from me, Tutt aimed and fired. He missed. I steadied my aim with my forearm and fired back. He was a dead man before he hit the ground."

"And you were acquitted in the inquiry that followed?"

"Of course."

Elliot took a deep breath and leaned back. He sensed he was getting at the truth of Wild Bill Hickok this morning. It excited him so much that he felt a need to slow down some to enable himself to absorb what he had just been told.

"Tell me, Bill. Do you think Custer can handle the Sioux?"

"If anyone can, he can."

"And if he does, do you think he may become our next president?"

"This country could do worse."

"It already has, with Grant," Elliot retorted mildly, finishing his drink.

Hickok shrugged and poured himself another. Elliot watched the man carefully for any sign that the rye he was consuming was having an effect on him, but Hickok seemed as steady as a rock.

Elliot cleared his throat. "Bill, as I understand it, the previous town marshal wore no gun and was successful in banning the carrying of sidearms within Abilene's town limits."

"You mean Bear River Tom?"

Elliot nodded in reply.

"And you wonder why I can't do the same." Bill's eyes gazed straight into Elliot's.

"Certainly there are many in Abilene who wonder that. My publisher, Miles Kramer, does. He mentioned it to me yesterday."

"Well, for one thing I am not Bear River Tom Smith. You might say it is a matter of style. He was a brute of a man with a mean pair of fists, an ex-New York policeman, if I am not mistaken. But if you will notice, he is no longer the town marshal. He was killed by a farmer with an ax."

"So I heard."

"I do not propose to let any man kill me with an ax or any other instrument, so I go armed. If people have a complaint, they should address it to the city council. Seems to me, my job would be a lot simpler if they banned the carrying of sidearms within the town's limits, and I promise you, if the town council passed such an ordinance, I would enforce it. But that's up to the city council." He drained his glass and slapped it down onto the table. "That clear enough for you, Elliot?"

"Of course. You are, after all, the creature of the city council."

"That's the way I see it."

"How many deputies do you have, Bill?"

"Counting Mike Williams, four in all. Champ Holler, Wilt Coffee, and Frank Ames are the others. Good

78

men, you'll find—not too quick on the trigger. I let them handle most of the trouble in town."

"Why is that?"

"Seems that whenever I get involved—a minor violation, a little spat over a girl, or a lush sleeping it off in a privy—it turns into a major event." He smiled wryly. "So I cut down my appearances, you might say."

"Except for this morning."

Hickok smiled and brushed back the hair that had fallen over his shoulder. "I must admit . . . I enjoyed that myself."

Elliot got to his feet.

"Thanks, Bill. This has been a most enlightening interview. I think you have been honest with me, and I appreciate it."

"Well, for an eastern reporter, you seem reasonable enough, Elliot. You don't seem to require whoppers to make you happy, and you ask intelligent questions."

As Elliot left the nearly empty saloon a moment later, he glanced back at Hickok. The man was still sitting with his back to the wall, completely alone, pouring himself another glass of rye. In that instant, Elliot felt a sudden stab of sympathy for the famous gunfighter. He looked so lonely and vulnerable, despite his flamboyant dress.

And something else: He looked very much like a target.

As the reporter disappeared out the door, Hickok heard the sharp click of a woman's heels coming at him from the rear of the saloon. He turned, expecting to see Jess Hazell, and saw instead an auburn-haired young girl who was only vaguely familiar. The moment he turned, the girl walked up hesitantly and smiled. In

79

that instant he recognized her as one of the women who had ridden into Abilene the day before on the same stage that had brought Agnes Thatcher and Jim Mulrey.

"You are Mr. Hickok, aren't you?" she inquired nervously.

He smiled to make it easier on her. "That's me. And who might you be, young lady?"

"I'm Sue Ann Mobley. Do you know where Mike is?"

"Mike Williams?"

"Yes, he told me last night that he's one of your deputies now. He was very pleased."

Hickok smiled. "He came to my aid at an opportune moment. He's a brave young man. Won't you join me?"

"Thank you," she said, walking around the table and sitting down.

"Would you care for a drink?"

"No, thank you. I came to find Mike, Mr. Hickok. I have something for him."

"I have no idea where he is at the moment. The last I saw, he was returning some paint we borrowed earlier."

"I wish I could wait," she said nervously. As she spoke, she reached into her pocketbook and took out some bills. "Here's six of the seven dollars Mike loaned me yesterday." She smoothed them on the table and pushed them toward Hickok. "My landlady has thrown me out. She found out that Mike is not my brother."

"And when she learned that, she decided you were not respectable, is that it?"

"I am afraid so."

Hickok looked dubiously at the bills. "I don't think Mike will need this money. And if I know him, he will want you to have it."

"No," she said, her small, pert chin suddenly as solid as granite. "I am going to find a job today and get a room of my own." She pushed the bills firmly all the way across the table to Hickok.

Reluctantly, he took the bills. "You are going to find a job? At what, Sue Ann?"

"I am going to be a dancer," she announced proudly. "I have very fine, solid calves and a good bust."

Hickok nodded sagely. "You do have a nice figure at that, but it might take more than a nice figure, Sue Ann."

"Not in this town. All the saloons want is someone for the cowboys to goggle at. I know that—I'm not so dumb."

"I guess not." Wild Bill looked down at his hands to keep from grinning.

"Do you know the owner of this saloon?"

"I do. His name is Patrick Kelly."

"Where might I find him?" Sue Ann asked.

"He's in his office now, I believe."

"Then I shall go see him."

"But the Alamo does not need dancers. It has an orchestra that plays almost around the clock."

"Then maybe it is time Mr. Kelly tried one or two dancers."

Certain now that no amount of good sense was going to stop this young lady, Hickok nodded and pointed to a door on the far side of the bar. "That's his office over there. Good luck, Sue Ann."

"Thank you," she said, getting up and marching directly for Kelly's office.

Watching her go, Hickok shook his head sadly. How many other young innocents like Sue Ann Mobley had he seen enter Abilene—each one with a head stuffed with the same foolish ambitions? These girls marched with such arrant gullibility into damnation that it was difficult for Hickok not to believe that this was their intention from the start.

As Sue Ann knocked at Kelly's office and then entered, Joe McCoy, the mayor of Abilene, pushed through the swinging doors and headed for Hickok. McCoy was a small, powerful man with shoulders as broad as a teamster's, jet-black hair, and an air of always being in a hurry. A more dynamic man Hickok had never met. At the moment the mayor was quite agitated, and Hickok thought he knew why: As one who had hired Hickok, McCoy felt he had the right to chastise the town marshal whenever he felt the occasion demanded it.

"What in blazes are you up to, Bill?" he wanted to know as he slumped into a chair at Hickok's table. "Are you trying to cut your own throat?"

"Slow down, Joe, slow down. Of course I ain't trying to cut my own throat."

"Then why have you seen fit to make an enemy of Ben Thompson?"

"You think I should have left that fool sign alone, do you?"

"Not exactly, but now we've got Thompson allied against us. We need his support if this town is to remain a cattle town."

"Joe," Hickok said patiently, leaning close, "you know perfectly well that I'm not taking sides in your dispute with the farmers and storekeepers. All I want is a safe, quiet town."

The man sighed wearily. "All right, Bill, all right. But I just want you to go slow if you can. Right now there's a Texan in back of Germano's barbershop with enough lead in him to make a horseshoe. Just try not to rely on those revolvers of yours so often, that's all."

"You're the second man today to suggest I should be another Bear River Tom Smith. If you don't like the way I keep peace in Abilene, Joe, hire someone else. Ben Thompson, for example. Or maybe Phil Coe."

"Now, now," the mayor cried, holding up his hand. "You know I don't mean that."

"Then let me drink in peace, Joe. I didn't enjoy last night, and this morning has me all stirred up. My nerves are shot, and I am trying to calm myself down. Let me be, will you?"

"Sure, Bill," the mayor said, getting to his feet. "I'll be in to see you later. You just go right ahead and calm down."

Hickok watched the mayor leave, then poured himself another drink. From the look of it, Abilene's days as a trail town were numbered. And if that were the case, what was to become of Wild Bill Hickok?

When Elliot returned to the newspaper office from his interview with Wild Bill, Connie left her desk and hurried over to him with a news item she had written during his absence. Sam Burgmeister, the printer, and two of his assistants, busy with the day's makeup, turned to watch as she handed him the copy.

"Mr. Burgmeister said I would have to get this cleared by you if it is to appear on the ladies' page." It was obvious she had not liked being overruled by the head pressman.

Frowning, Elliot took it from her. "What is this?"

"Read it, Elliot."

He did and was astonished. It was an account of the deflowering of Ben Thompson's bull, and it was a model of restraint. At the same time it clearly communicated the frustration so many women of Abilene must have felt for so long because of the sign. Also, Connie

83

had been most appreciative of and quite fair in her treatment of Hickok's handling of the matter.

Glancing up from the article, Elliot smiled. "I could not have written it any better, Connie. You have a natural talent for the pen."

"I was on hand to witness the event for myself, Elliot. You are not angry?"

"I was perhaps a bit of a prig, I must admit. It is clear from the way you have handled this that smut is in the eye of the beholder." He smiled. "Tell Sam I think it would go nicely on the front page. No reason to hide so newsworthy an item on a back page."

Connie glowed. "I saw you walk off with Mr. Hickok. Did you get much from him?"

"Too much, I am afraid."

"Why, what do you mean by that?"

"What he had to say was sobering, to say the least. He is not the Wild Bill that legend would have it, I am afraid—just a very tough man in an exceedingly tough job. I must admit, I feel only sympathy for him. Does that seem odd to you?"

"No," she said. "That seems perfectly human."

At that moment a farmer strode into the *Chronicle* office, dressed in his Sunday suit. A big, powerful man with broad shoulders, he had the unmistakable look of the soil about him, with rough, callused hands and fingernails as black as his eyes, which now peered warily around the office. He was obviously not a town man—closed-in places seemed to worry him.

As soon as he caught sight of Elliot and Connie, he pushed himself through the low gate and walked toward them, the pungent smell of hayseed and freshly turned soil clinging stubbornly to him.

"Name's Jud Powell," he said, sticking out his hand. "I reckon you'd be the new editor. Miles Kramer told me to come see you."

Elliot's knuckles grated painfully as Powell grasped his hand and shook it enthusiastically. "What can I do for you?" Elliot asked.

"I think I have news you'll want to print. It concerns the future of Abilene."

"Excuse me, Elliot," Connie said, moving away. "I'll take this copy over to Sam now."

Elliot nodded to her, then led the farmer into his new office, where the upper walls were glassed in. Elliot had not yet had time even to sit in the leather swivel chair behind the flat-topped desk.

"Sit down, Mr. Powell," he said, waving at a wooden, straight-backed chair by the desk, "and tell me just what this news of yours is."

The big farmer sat down and smiled at Elliot with some pride. "You are looking at the recently elected president of the Farmers' Protective Association, Mr. Carson."

Elliot leaned back in his swivel chair. "Congratulations, Mr. Powell. But I have a suspicion there's more to it than that simple announcement."

"There sure as shootin' is," the granger replied. "We farmers have organized for one reason: to get rid of the cattle trade. We intend to see to it that the Texas cattle trade is outlawed."

Elliot smiled. "And just how do you plan to do that?"

"There will be elections for the town council soon. We will elect men favorable to our cause, then pass an ordinance making the cattle trade illegal in Abilene."

"As simple as that?"

"Yes, Mr. Carson. As simple as that."

"But isn't the cattle trade the source of Abilene's wealth?"

"It was, but it need not be. Not any longer."

"Then Abilene does not need the extra wealth?"

Powell smiled at Elliot patiently. "We farmers spend a considerable sum in Abilene, Mr. Carson. And the money we bring to Abilene will not come tainted."

"As is the money that comes from the cattle trade."

"Precisely, Mr. Carson."

"Such a course as you describe will not be easy, you understand."

Powell nodded emphatically. "We expect opposition. The elections will be hard fought. But even so, there is always the chance that the present city council will outlaw the cattle trade on its own. The handwriting is on the wall, Mr. Carson."

"It certainly won't be the same Abilene," Elliot remarked, bemused. "Without the cattle trade, I mean."

"That is exactly our purpose."

"But where will the Texans go to ship their cattle?"

"There's a new town abuilding south of here—in Harvey County. Newton, it's called."

"And your complaints, specifically, are . . . ?"

"The trail herds make no effort to go around our fields. These Texans have nothing but contempt for us and treat us accordingly. Just last week Wallace Rugger, a farmer only a few miles from me, was pistol-whipped by a Texan for trying to chase off a longhorn steer that had taken over his front yard."

"Suppose the Texas cowboys agreed to stop doing that."

"You might as well plead with the devil to give up trapping men's souls. And deviling farmers is what those Texans do best, Mr. Carson. They regard themselves as mounted knights, while to them we are not fit to place fodder before their steeds. I would hold no stock at all in any such agreement." Powell leaned back in his chair. "No, Mr. Carson, enough is enough. We are standing together and will not rest until we have driven this pestilence from our land. Locusts at least give us a six-year respite. From this plague of cattle and horsemen, there is no rest at all."

"And what you want from the *Chronicle* is news of your organization."

"And its goals."

"You want to stir things up."

"We need to gain allies in Abilene. We know of no better way than to advertise our intentions. An organization that is not known has little power of persuasion. We have no doubt our plans will arouse opposition, but we are equally certain there are many in Abilene who are as determined as we are to clean it up. I might add that T. C. Henry, one of the founders of Abilene, is in our corner. He plans to throw his full weight behind our cause."

Rapping on the glass, Elliot beckoned to Connie, who left her desk and hurried into his office. Introducing Connie to Powell, he briefly went over with her what he and Jud Powell had been discussing and suggested that Connie might want to take down all the pertinent information from Powell and work it into a story. Then smiling at her, Elliot said it might be nice to see the new article placed on the front page, alongside her account of the activities outside the Bull's Head that morning. He was sure their readers would not miss the significance of such a placement.

"Think you can handle that, Miss Witherspoon?"

Connie was delighted. "Of course, Elliot," she told him. Then she looked down with a smile at the big farmer. "Come right this way, Mr. Powell."

As Connie led the farmer over to her desk, Elliot left the *Chronicle* office and headed for the barbershop, where the Texan that Wild Bill had wounded was being treated. It had dawned on the editor that the account of last night's shoot-out in the Bull's Head also deserved a prominent place on the *Chronicle*'s front page. This was to be his first issue, and Elliot was anxious to make it one the entire community of Abilene would remember.

Chapter 6

A cheerful grin on his face, Mike Williams—standing on the bank of the Smoky Hill River just outside of town—swiftly drew both his Remingtons and fired from the hip. The can went dancing merrily along the ground toward the river. After six shots, Mike spun both revolvers back into their holsters, then peered up through the smoke at Hickok for approval.

Waving away the smoke, Hickok took one of Mike's Remingtons from him and hefted it. He shook his head slightly, dissatisfied with the balance. "The Remington is a heavy, unbalanced weapon, Mike, but there are those who swear by it. Jesse James's brother, Frank, likes it, for one. And I must admit—you just showed me some fine shooting. You made that tin can dance a jig, and that's a fact. But why don't you try my Colt and see what you think?"

Blushing with pleasure at Hickok's compliment, Mike took the marshal's Colt, examined it for a moment, and still aiming from the hip, began firing. Just as before, the hapless can was kicked ahead by the singing slugs until it went popping into the Smoky Hill River. By that time the smoke was so heavy both men had to turn their faces away.

When the smoke finally cleared, Wild Bill caught

sight of Agnes Thatcher, still waiting patiently for them in the rented buggy, and waved to her. Smiling, she waved back, her pink parasol resting on her shoulder.

Hickok looked back at Mike. "Well, how did it feel?"

"The Colt's a lot more comfortable," Mike admitted.

"One other thing, Mike. Why do you draw your weapons so fast and shoot from the hip? You seem to put a lot of store by that."

"I sure do, Bill. In a tight situation, a fast draw might save my life."

"I admit that," Hickok replied, nodding his head. "There are times when a fast draw is important. But you shouldn't let yourself get into that kind of a pickle to begin with. Most of the time you should know trouble is coming and have your gun out and ready to fire. Sure, it's pretty to see a man fire from the hip, and the crowds love it at circuses and shooting exhibitions, but it's also a damn good way to miss what you're aiming at."

"You mean you aim all the time?"

"As often as I can. And usually I steady my weapon with my left forearm—like this." As he spoke, he suited action to words. Using his left forearm to steady his Colt, he fired at a twig growing out of a tree stump along the embankment. There was only one shot left in the cylinder, but that single bullet was good enough, and the twig vanished.

Mike was impressed. "That was fine shooting, Bill."

"It was quick, too. A fast draw isn't always necessary, Mike. But, of course, a sidearm is best fired rapidly and at short ranges—and you must not hesitate. While you're considering, the other man might be killing you. Remember that."

"I will," Mike said solemnly. "I guess you didn't

hesitate much when you caught that Texan last week in the Bull's Head."

"That's right, Mike. I didn't. Maybe if I had, he wouldn't still be suffering like he is. The thing is, I was shooting blindly in the dark at the time and could not aim for any particular spot. I hope you never have to shoot any man, Mike, but if you do, catch him in the gut, near the navel. You may not make a fatal shot, but it should paralyze his brain and arm so much the fight will be over."

At that moment three surreys packed with men and women swept on past the rented buggy and turned abruptly, pulling up ten or twenty yards farther along the bank. Even before the crowded surreys had come to a complete halt, their occupants poured from them, heading for the river.

Undressing with reckless haste, some of them plunged naked into the water. The rest, too drunk to undress, simply followed their companions blindly, plunging into the river fully clothed, adding to the general hilarity. Splashing merrily about in the water, men were helping the women undress, while the women undressed the men.

The entire scene was accompanied by delighted shrieks and uproarious laughter. Staggering around hip deep in the water, whiskey flasks gleaming in the morning sunlight, the bathers passed the alcohol back and forth, the naked women snatching for it as eagerly as the men. After several moments, a few of the revelers, drenched and hilarious, chased each other up onto the bank for further diversions.

Watching their escapades, Hickok chuckled. It was like a scene from a Renaissance painting he had noticed once, on a rich Denver art collector's wall, in which a few overripe nymphs and bearded satyrs chased each other over the bucolic landscape. As Hickok remembered it, the hollows and grassy lawns had been alive with couples who had already managed to catch each other.

"Them would be Ruby Winstead's girls," he told Mike, "and some of their choice male customers. Looks like they decided to keep last night's party going awhile longer."

"I guess we better get on back," Mike said. He had been watching, wide-eyed. "I don't reckon this is something Agnes would want to see. I hope she's not offended."

"Don't worry about her," Hickok said with a laugh. "I am sure Agnes knows such things happen."

Abruptly, Mike halted, his face as pale as a bedsheet. Hickok walked on for a moment, then noticed Mike's absence next to him, and turned.

"What's wrong, Mike?"

Pointing at some women and men still splashing about in the water, he said, "It's Sue Ann!"

Hickok looked toward the river.

"She's there! I can see her! With those two men in the water!"

Peering carefully, Hickok was able to make out the slim figure of the young girl who one week before had told him she was going to be a dancer. He was now able to see that she had the hips for a professional dancer— but little else. She had found proper employment, it seemed . . . the only course open to her in this town. It was sad but not unexpected.

"Oh, my God, Bill! Look at her!"

Hickok put an arm around his newest deputy. "Easy does it, Mike. It's her choice to make."

But Mike was already on his way to the frolicking crowd on the bank. Abruptly, he began to run. Hickok took after him, swearing softly, but before he could overtake Mike, the distraught young man had waded into the water and grabbed Sue Ann's arm.

Fluttering and squalling like a wet hen, she was dragged from the water by Mike, and the moment they reached the shore, he tore off his coat and flung it around the girl's bony nakedness.

"See here!" the Texan with Sue Ann cried. "That's our girl. We already done paid up for her. Go get your own!" The big naked man tried to pull Mike away from Sue Ann, but Mike clubbed at him wildly, catching him on the side of the head. The blow sent him stumbling backward into the water just as Wild Bill reached the river's bank. Instantly Mike and the marshal found themselves surrounded by crazed, dripping men—each as naked as a jaybird.

Hickok had once read a book in which a man called Gulliver had encountered humans resembling apes. They had sprung into the trees on Gulliver's approach and urinated down upon him. It was a fanciful tale, but there was nothing fanciful about the furious, naked apes crouching about Mike and Hickok at that moment. Bent forward, mouths slack with drink, eyes wild, some of them with their knuckles brushing the ground, they looked ready to spring.

"You Yankees want ever'thing!" cried one of them. "Well, maybe we'll just send you all floating down that river!"

"That's right!" cried another. "Belly up!"

The men moved closer. Hickok felt the hackles rising on the back of his neck as he drew both revolvers. Sue Ann was staring around her, wide-eyed and fearful. Aiming carefully, Hickok sent a shot whispering just over the closest Texan's head. The naked man leaped away, and the rest cringed back as well. Slowly, Hickok turned around, meeting each man's eye. That was enough: The men were naked . . . helpless . . . and drunk to boot. They fell quickly back, their eyes no longer meeting the marshal's.

Hickok turned to Mike. "Let's go. There's nothing more you can do here. These men are outside the town's limits, and we have no jurisdiction."

"I am going to take Sue Ann back with me."

"No, you aren't!" Sue Ann cried out in sudden exasperation, her voice clear and defiant. "You got no right to come here and tell me what to do. You don't own me, Mike Williams! I can do whatever I want to do!"

"But, Sue Ann! . . ."

"Never you mind!" she cried, flinging the coat back at him. "You aren't my pap! You aren't my kin. And Miss Ruby's treating me real nice. Leave me be, I say! It's too late now! I don't have anyplace left to go!"

Abruptly, she collapsed to the ground, sobbing.

Hickok turned Mike around and nudged him back toward their buggy. Grudgingly, eyes still filled with hatred, the naked Texans moved aside to let them through. Mike walked on ahead of Hickok without further protest, the picture of a beaten man. When he reached the buggy, Agnes helped him up beside her as Hickok took the reins.

Even before Wild Bill started up the team, the sound of renewed merriment exploded from the riverbank.

Hickok, leaning back in his chair, smiled as Major Farber leaned forward to rake in his winnings. The major gave Hickok the impression of a man who would always manage somehow to recover for one more throw of the dice or one more drink on the house. He knew how to win without boasting and how to lose with equal grace. Because he was enjoying a phenomenal run of luck at the moment, the major was trying to rein in his natural exuberance out of respect for those at the table who were losing. But the unmistakable light of triumph shone in the old campaigner's eyes, and for Hickok it was a pleasure to see. There were damn few times in a man's life when he knew he had all the cards. When a moment like that did come, a fellow had every right to savor it.

"I must admit, Major," Hickok said, "it looks like you've got the cards today." He pushed the pack toward the man. "Your deal."

The major shook his head. "It has been a long and profitable afternoon, Bill, but the time has come for me to call a halt. This day's game of chance has ended. I shall pause on the crest for once, rather than in the depths of the trough. Too often, it seems, we wait until we are plunging down the far side of our fortune before taking stock."

"That's all right with me, Major," replied Hickok, smiling. "Take all the stock you want."

"Fine! I might add that at the moment I am as dry as a bone bleaching in the Kansas sun. I crave liquid nourishment. Allow me to purchase drinks for the table before I move on."

"Thank you," said Hickok. "That's decent of you."

The other two players looked at each other and shrugged. They would have no chance to win back what they had lost, but with the major's phenomenal luck, there would not have been any chance of that, anyway. Not today, at any rate. The two men brightened somewhat and thanked the major.

As Major Farber called to the barmaid, Hickok glanced over at the table where he had left Mike Williams earlier that evening. Mike was still there, his head slumped down upon the table. Hickok was not surprised: Mike had been drinking steadily since they returned from the river that morning.

The drinks arrived, Hickok's a rye, with whiskey for the others. After the four men toasted each other and drank up, the major bid them good-bye and headed for the bar to cash in his chips.

Hickok decided to call it an evening, excused himself, and left the table, heading for the drink-sodden Mike Williams. Even before he reached him, Hickok could smell his youngest deputy.

"Mike," Hickok said softly, taking him by the shoulder and shaking him gently.

Mike stirred fitfully, then lapsed back into his alcoholic stupor. Hickok straightened and beckoned to one of the barkeeps, the one used primarily as a bouncer. His name was Butterfield, and he was huge. To get in the Alamo's back door, Butterfield had to stoop, and there were some in Abilene who swore his eyelids had muscles. When the bouncer arrived, Hickok asked him to help with Mike.

Nodding amiably, Butterfield bent quickly, flung the unconscious man over his shoulder as casually as he would a mop handle, and turned to Hickok. "Lead the way, Bill."

Hickok held the rear door open for the barkeep, then preceded him down the alley until they came to Mike's rooming house. He was glad Mike's landlady did not appear as he led the way up to Mike's room on the second floor. Pushing open the door, he stood aside for the big Butterfield, who with surprising gentleness let Mike down on the quilted bed and stepped back.

"He's had a snootful, that's for sure," Butterfield said, and then he shook his head. "He's an awful young man to carry that much whiskey and that much artillery. You take good care of him, Bill. Hear?"

"I hear," said Hickok. "Thanks, Butterfield."

The man nodded and vanished, his footsteps on the stairs falling as lightly as a girl's. Closing the door,

Hickok walked over to his inebriated friend and attempted to wake him, but Mike was out completely. Not bothering to light a lamp, Hickok pulled off Mike's boots, loosened his string tie, drew off his coat, and threw a blanket over him.

Mike was snoring with his mouth wide open when Hickok shut the door and descended the stairs.

On his way back to the Alamo, Hickok was careful not to use the same alley he had taken to Mike's rooming house. Stepping off the sidewalk, he moved out into the street until he was walking down the middle of the wide thoroughfare. It was such an ingrained habit for him to keep plenty of open space around him when he was outside that he did it without thinking, waving absently to those horsemen and buggies that were forced to slow down to skirt his solitary figure.

As he trudged along, his thoughts fled back to that small room where Mike lay, sodden with whiskey. That Mike had fallen for that young gal was understandable—she surely was pretty enough—but that did not make it any less of a mistake. If Mike proved unable to shake off his yen for Sue Ann, only trouble lay ahead for both of them.

When the Alamo was looming before him, Wild Bill left the street and headed for it. Just as he was passing the mouth of the alley adjacent to the saloon, the marshal thought he glimpsed something gleaming, as if of metal. He swung to face it at the same moment that the darkness exploded in a gunflash, and a bullet snicked off a piece of his right sleeve. Both Colts drawn now, Hickok went down on one knee and triggered three quick shots into the alley.

There was no answering fire.

Without hesitation, Hickok plunged into the alley after his would-be assassin. Spying a small figure ducking around the corner ahead of him, he increased his speed, and when he rounded the corner, he saw the man racing down another alley. The light was too poor and the distance too great to chance a shot, so Hickok continued to race after the fleeing figure.

A moment later, having crossed two alleys and two side streets, the marshal pulled up in frustration. There was no sign of his quarry. He turned around and started back, not failing to note as he did that he was passing the rear of the Bull's Head saloon.

Pushing through the crowd that had gathered at the head of the alley, Hickok entered the Alamo. Major Horace Farber was standing just inside the door, apparently waiting for him.

"I must speak to you, sir," the major whispered anxiously.

With a curt nod of his head, Hickok indicated his customary table at the back of the Alamo and proceeded toward it, the major keeping close behind him. By this time every person in the saloon knew of the attempt on Hickok's life, and every eye was fixed on him. Even the barkeeps—in the act of serving customers when he entered—were now simply watching.

No one made any effort to speak to him or ask a question, however. By this time the citizens of Abilene knew enough to keep their distance whenever Hickok was involved in a shooting—especially when he was the target.

"What do you want, Major?" Hickok asked, slumping into his chair, his cold eyes sweeping the bar and dance hall. Not a single person met his gaze without flinching away. At once, the Alamo's patrons turned back to the bar, the gaming picked up where it had left off, and the orchestra resumed playing.

The major cleared his throat nervously. "Did you happen to get a look at the man who shot at you?"

"Too dark."

"I think I know who it was."

Hickok was busy reloading one of his Colts, but he glanced up. "Go on, Major."

"It was that surly cur who arrived on the stage with us a week ago."

"Mulrey," Hickok said flatly, without surprise.

"Yes."

"You saw him in the alley with his gun out."

"No, I was on my way out of the Alamo, and Mulrey was on the porch peering in here. It has been my misfortune to have played poker with him and his fellows at the Bull's Head, and I was forced to take his paper for a not inconsiderable sum."

"Go on, Major," Hickok said patiently.

"Well, sir, I nodded to the man, and as I attempted to move on past him, he stuck his feral face inches from mine and hissed that this would be the last time I would play poker with you." The major paused delicately. "He did not refer to you by name, Bill, I must admit, but as 'that long-haired bastard.' Then he turned away."

"You mean he did not threaten me by name?" Hickok inquired, an ironic smile lighting his grim features.

"Not by name. But we both know to whom the blackguard was referring."

"Yes, we both know—but this is not proof I can use in a court of law, Major."

"I am well aware of that lamentable fact, Bill. My purpose at this moment is to warn you. Mulrey, I am sure, is your would-be assassin. Forewarned is forearmed, as I understand it."

"Quite right, and thank you, Major. I will not forget this."

As Hickok spoke, he stuck his reloaded Colt into

his sash and stood up. The moment he did so, the orchestra's members stopped playing again, and the men at the bar turned to watch. As the roulette wheel clicked to a slow halt, the craps table went silent.

Glancing down at the major, Hickok spoke again. "You say Mulrey frequents the Bull's Head?"

The major nodded, and without another word, Hickok left the table and strode from the Alamo into the dimly lit streets of Abilene.

He was almost to the Bull's Head when Elliot Carson, in his shirt sleeves and almost completely out of breath, ran up and exclaimed, "Bill, I just heard about the shooting!"

Hickok stopped walking, and instantly the crowd that had been gathering on both sides of the street halted as well. Not a single person ventured out onto the broad street where Hickok and Elliot were standing, though.

"What can you tell me?" Elliot asked anxiously.

Hickok indicated the hole in his sleeve with a glance. "Someone took a shot at me. It could have been someone else he was aiming at," he drawled, "but it was me he came closest to hitting."

"This is terrible, Bill. Who was it?"

"I am not sure."

"But you must suspect someone."

Hickok nodded his assent. "Oh, I do, but I wouldn't want to accuse anyone without proof for you to splash it all over your paper. You've already got the Texans riled up enough the way you've been pushing that farmers' association."

"Then you think it's a Texan."

"Didn't say that. Didn't mean that. Move off, Elliot. I got business. This street is dark, there's an alley at my back, and you're standing right next to me. The next bullet might miss me and hit you."

"Dammit, Bill, I am not asking as the editor of the *Chronicle*, but as your friend. I am concerned for your safety."

Hickok smiled with sudden warmth and clapped Elliot on the shoulder. "So am I, Elliot, and I appreciate your concern. Now go on back to your newspaper and let me do what I can to resolve the situation."

With a curt nod, the marshal moved off, continuing on down the center of the street toward the Bull's Head. The crowd on the sidewalks followed in an uncanny silence. The scene was almost as unsettling as the knowledge that a whiskey-crazed Mulrey could well be aiming another six-gun at his back.

Reaching the Bull's Head, Hickok drew both guns, mounted the steps, and pushed through the swinging doors. The damage to the place incurred during the confrontation over the saloon's controversial sign had been completely repaired. Nevertheless, in contrast to the Alamo, the Bull's Head was still a dark place, rank with the stench of cigar smoke, sweaty bodies, and unwashed feet. The floor was covered with sawdust that might have been fresh a week ago, and along the right wall ran the bar. Poker tables were set along the left wall. The stairway up which Hickok had raced to defend Joe Taylor from the Texan was just beyond the bar. There was no orchestra, and a tiny dance floor in the back was cluttered with gaming tables. The only light in the place was shed by smoky lamps set on a wagon wheel suspended from the ceiling.

The patrons of the place were waiting for Hickok. Most if not all of the men were Texans. Leaning with his back to the bar and standing alongside Ben Thompson was Jim Mulrey, looking as guilty as a fox with a mouthful of chicken feathers. As Hickok approached him, sweat poured down Mulrey's unshaven face, washing it lighter in ragged streaks.

Sitting at a table with Phil Coe hovering over her, Jess Hazell said, "Hello, Bill. Ain't seen you much lately."

Hickok glanced at her. "That's been your choice, Jess. You know where to find me."

"Sure I do—at the Alamo," she said, "with your highfalutin lady friends."

Hickok knew she meant Agnes Thatcher, and he was puzzled. Seldom had he been to the Alamo with Agnes; he had taken the woman out only one or two times in the past week, not including this day's unlucky ride out to the river.

"I'm not complaining, Jess," Hickok told her. "Like you said, you've got a right to cut your cards wherever you choose. If this is where you want to play your hand out, suits me."

A desolate look flooded Jess's eyes. She was about to say something to him but decided now was not the time for this conversation. The next moment Hickok turned abruptly to Jim Mulrey.

"Come out now, Mulrey, and finish what you started. I'll be waiting."

The man looked frantically around him for help, then addressed Hickok, his voice quavering. "What you sayin' that for, Marshal? That's downright provokin'. You tryin' to start something?"

"Look, Mulrey, I'll give you time to draw and fire, if that's what's bothering your yellow hide. Any distance you want—but it'll be out in the street . . . in the open . . . where everyone can watch." Hickok smiled thinly. "There's a crowd out there now, waiting."

"Leave him be, Bill," Ben Thompson said, stepping away from the bar and planting himself squarely between Hickok and Mulrey. "He ain't done nothin'. You're just upset because someone took a shot at you tonight. Could've been anyone in this room, as a matter of fact—everyone except poor Mulrey here, 'cause he's been with me. Besides, ain't you satisfied you got one man wishes he were dead right now thrashing around in the back of the barbershop?"

"You heard him!" Mulrey cried, frantically grasping at the alibi Thompson had given him. "It's the truth! I ain't been out of this place all night!" Mulrey turned to the room full of Texans. "Ain't that right, fellers? Ain't I been here all along?"

Every man in the place nodded solemnly, and each face that Hickok studied told him it was a lie. A few didn't even bother to keep their faces straight. They were Texans, and they were thinking of their fellow Texan who was taking a god-awful long time to die.

Hickok looked at Phil Coe, who still sat close to Jess Hazell. "What about it, Phil? You sayin' Mulrey was in here all night?"

"That's right, Bill. Mulrey's been here all night— just like me and Jess here." He snaked his arm around Jess's shoulders, pulling her toward him.

Hickok nodded, then looked at Jess. Apparently shaken, she looked quickly away and, sitting forward, snatched at her drink with one hand, the long fingers of the other moving nervously through her red curls. She could not meet his gaze. She still cared enough, he realized, not to lie to him.

"I thank you for not lying to me, Jess," Hickok said, "but I sure don't understand how you can stand the stench of your new friends. If this bushwhacking pack of killers is what you want, you're welcome to them."

"Damn you, Bill!" Coe snarled, jumping to his feet so suddenly that his chair tipped over behind him. "I ain't gonna sit here and let you bad-mouth me and my friends!"

Like a pack of wolves getting ready to pounce, the

men in the place, including Coe, took a step closer to Hickok, hands resting lightly on the grips of holstered six-guns.

What was needed, the marshal realized, was a diversion.

Hickok slapped Coe hard, catching him on the side of the head and sending him hurtling backward to the floor. As Coe struck it, his elbow knocked a full cuspidor, spilling its contents over his arm and chest. Seething, his blood-red lips twisting in shame and rage, Coe glared up at Hickok, his gun hand reaching back for his weapon. Hickok smiled and waited for the draw, but Coe—beside himself though he was—made no effort to stand up or to go for his weapon. He did not fancy committing suicide that night.

"That's right, Coe," Hickok said calmly, smiling down contemptuously at the man. "Lie in that slop. It's where you belong."

Then the marshal turned his back boldly on the crowded saloon and strode out the doors. The waiting crowd on the street melted back into the darkness as soon as they saw Hickok leave the place unscathed. He might have been mistaken, but Hickok thought he even heard a few sighs of disappointment. He stood for a moment on the veranda, staring icily at the crowd, waiting for it to disperse, and when it finally did, he started down the steps.

He had just reached the street when he heard the saloon doors behind him swing open.

"Bill!"

Hickok turned to see Jess hurrying down the stairs toward him, and he waited for her.

Slowing up in front of him, Jess sagged against him, resting her forehead on his chest. "Oh, Bill, I'm sorry, but I couldn't lie to you. I couldn't."

"I'm glad you didn't, Jess," he said, stroking her red curls. "I appreciate it."

She stepped back and looked up into his face. In the depths of her pleading eyes, he saw tears shimmering. "Bill, you must get out of Abilene. They'll kill you! Especially now, after what you did in there tonight."

"Your friend Coe will kill me?"

"He's not my friend, Bill. You know me better than that!"

"I thought I did, Jess . . . but now I'm not so sure."

"Well, what about *your* fine friend?"

"That's all she is, Jess—a friend. I met Agnes and her husband a few years back. I helped out his circus once by putting on a shooting exhibition."

"So now she shows up here . . . looking for you."

"I never had much luck telling a woman what to do, Jess. It's a free country. Anyone who wants to come to Abilene is welcome to do so, long as they don't break any laws."

"But you've been seeing her."

"Hell, Jess, by holing up in this here bullpen, you haven't given me much choice, have you?"

Then he turned and walked off. He heard her call out to him once more, but he kept on walking.

Chapter 7

Elliot Carson—more interested in how well Connie rode sidesaddle than he was in the surrounding countryside—was taken by surprise when Jud Powell, astride one of his own workhorses just ahead, called back to him, "Look there, behind the barn!"

Jud had just topped a ridge and was pointing to a small farm less than a mile ahead of them. Reining up, Elliot stood in his stirrups and saw a herd of longhorns milling about in a small depression behind the farm buildings. And then he saw what had drawn the cattle— they were drinking at the farmer's pond.

"What is it, Elliot?" Connie asked, pulling up beside him.

Elliot sat back down into his saddle. "Looks like a whole herd's drinking up that farmer's pond."

Spurring their horses forward, Elliot and Connie galloped up beside Jud.

"Whose farm is that?" Elliot asked.

"Tom Bonwell's," Jud told them, his voice full of gloom.

"Those steers are going to drain the pond. There's too many of them."

"And that's only part of it," Jud said.

"What's the rest of it?" Connie wanted to know.

"Look around you. See those fields of wheat over there? And look beyond, to that rye field in the distance."

Connie gazed where Jud Powell had directed. "They look trampled."

"They are," he replied.

"Then how is he going to harvest his crop?"

"Don't look like he is now."

"This is terrible," Connie said. "Why doesn't the farmer chase these cattle off his land? It is his land, isn't it?"

"Of course it's his land," said Jud. "But what choice does he have? Look closely at that herd."

Elliot and Connie squinted to get a better focus and were able to make out the dim, dust-shrouded figures of horsemen—Texas cowboys, they had no doubt—wheeling their mounts in and out of the herd in an effort to keep the longhorns from breaking away.

Of course, Elliot thought. Each one of those Texans was armed. And as Jud had been telling him, to a Texan any land his horse could take him over was his land, to be used as he saw fit. And right now that farm pond belonging to Tom Bonwell was being used as those Texans saw fit. Confronted with such a combination of arrogance and firepower, there was precious little a peaceful farmer could do.

Elliot had heard Jud tell of it, but seeing it first-hand was making a much stronger impression. To witness this sort of thing was obviously why Jud had invited the two of them to visit his farm today and go riding with him.

"You'd better stay here," Elliot said to Connie. Then he glanced at the president of the new grangers' association. "Let's go, Jud."

"I'm not staying behind, Elliot!" Connie announced.

In a way Elliot had expected just that response.

"Come ahead then," he called over his shoulder to her.
"But stay close!"

A moment later the three of them were spurring
their horses across the field toward Tom Bonwell's farm.

Distances on this Kansas prairie were deceptive.
Only after a few minutes of steady galloping was Elliot
able to make out the small huddle of people standing
together in front of the farmhouse. As he rode closer,
he made out the figure of a woman, her husband, and
two children. A horseman was cantering away from
their yard, heading toward Elliot and his companions.

When the rider got close enough, he pulled up and
grinned at the three of them. One look at the work-
horse Jud was riding and he started to laugh. He seemed
to be a good-natured fellow, but he had the light blue
eyes that Elliot had come to associate with a careless,
almost criminal contempt for any kind of restraint.

"Where in hell are you three going?" the Texan
wanted to know.

"To the Bonwell place," Jud replied.

"Well, why are you in such an all-fired hurry to get
there?"

"That's none of your damned business," said Elliot.
He felt anger rocking through him and was astonished
to feel himself react in this fashion.

"Oh, now, what's this?" the cowboy asked, cross-
ing his arms casually over his saddle horn. "You itchin'
for trouble, mister?"

"Seems to me you're the one looking for trouble,"
snapped Connie. "I suggest you move aside and allow
us to ride on to the Bonwell house. Unless, of course,
you've decided to take that over as well as their pond."

The Texan was obliged to touch his hat brim to
Connie—it was a part of his upbringing and died hard.
Swallowing his anger some, he pulled his horse back

out of their path, saying in an exaggerated drawl, "Why, yes indeed, ma'am. Ride on through. I am sure the Bonwells will be delighted to see you."

Using her riding crop, Connie urged her horse to a lope and moved swiftly past the cowboy. As Jud and then Elliot followed, the Texan turned in beside Elliot, reached over, and snatched the reins from his hand; then wheeling swiftly, he yanked Elliot's mount completely around. So taken by surprise was Elliot that he was unable to prevent himself from flying backward out of his saddle. With a triumphant hoot, the cowboy galloped off with Elliot's horse.

Connie, hearing the cowboy's cry, slowed her horse to look back. Elliot was scrambling to his feet and cursing violently. Jud Powell pulled his horse around, galloped back, and reaching down, helped Elliot up behind him. Still muttering oaths, Elliot clasped Jud around the waist and hung on. It was in this fashion that the three of them rode the rest of the way to the Bonwell place.

A half an hour later, the five of them—Tom and Louise Bonwell, Elliot, Connie, and Jud—were in the Bonwell kitchen. The two Bonwell children—a tow-headed boy and a flaxen-haired girl—had insisted on staying outside to watch the cowboys. The farmhouse was a solid, long-sided structure, but the bawling of the cattle in back of the barn came through the walls clearly.

A fresh pot of coffee in her hand, Louise Bonwell hurried over from the stove. She was a skinny, blond woman with high cheekbones and skin so pale it looked like fresh milk.

"I'm just so mortified," she said, shaking her head in dismay as she poured the coffee. "Those awful men have been here with their herd since before breakfast. Tom says the steers are breaking down the pond's embankment, and if they don't leave soon, the pond will be gone."

Her husband spoke up then, his voice bitter. "Shoot, Louise, that pond's gone already. It won't be nothing but a hog wallow when those steers get through. It's too late to save it."

Shaking his head bitterly, he sipped the scalding coffee. Bonwell appeared to be in his early thirties and looked about five years older than his wife. He was a sturdy, tanned farmer with keen blue eyes, but what Elliot had noticed about him first thing was the hopeless sag to his shoulders, which made him appear just about ready to turn tail and run.

"Now listen you two," Jud said urgently. "Don't let them Texans chase you off your homestead. There are people in Abilene who are beginning to side with us. The day will come when no more trail herds will be making their way to Abilene—when Abilene will be a quiet farming community." Jud turned to Elliot. "Ain't that right, Elliot?"

"I know that's what you'd like," Elliot admitted, "but that day hasn't come yet. Still, after seeing firsthand what you farmers out here have to put up with, I can tell you one thing for certain. The *Chronicle* will do what it can."

"Hear that?" Jud said to the Bonwells. "Once we get public opinion behind us, there'll be no way this damned cattle trade can go on."

"That's what you said when you helped form the Farmers' Protective Association a month ago, Jud. All we've done so far is make up petitions."

"That was only two weeks ago, Tom, and those petitions are still making the rounds. But in the meantime we need candidates to run for the town council. Rome wasn't built in a day."

"I know that, Jud," Tom said. "I don't mean to find

fault. But I got troubles right now, as you can see. Half my crop is ruined—most of my wheat and better than half of my rye."

Standing behind Jud's chair, Louise rested her hand on her husband's shoulder to comfort him and then looked unhappily at Elliot and Connie. "We've both worked so hard. Last year the trail herders didn't bother us, so we thought we were too far out from Abilene to worry about their cattle. But now, everything we've done all spring is being trampled into the ground—all in one day."

Connie spoke up then. "You say the trail herd got here this morning?"

Louise nodded and slumped down at the table beside her husband. "We heard shots and went outside, but we couldn't see anyone. The shots were coming from behind the barn, so Tom loaded up his shotgun and went to investigate."

"It was these damn Texans," Tom went on grimly. "Announcing their presence, they were. Some of them had set tin cans on top of my fence posts and were shooting them off. And behind them came the trail herd."

"When Tom asked them to stop shooting at the posts," Louise continued, "and told them that he had two small children on the farm, they just laughed at him and began shooting at his feet."

"They made me dance, all right. Yes, sir, they sure did. Louise came running and that shamed them some, so they holstered their weapons. But they didn't stop their cattle from spreading out all over my fields and crowding into the pond." He shook his head bitterly and ran his hand through his hair. "What could I do? I couldn't hope to shoot all of them. I had to stand there and let them do whatever they wanted—*on my land*."

The room became silent then, as each person in it

111

contemplated the humiliation suffered by Tom Bonwell this day. Before his wife and children, he had been forced to back off and acquiesce to what amounted to a rape of his farm by these arrogant, unprincipled cowboys from the south.

The sudden clatter of hooves filled the room as horsemen rode up to the cabin. At the same time, the door burst open and in raced the two children.

"The cowboys are coming!" the boy shouted. "All of them!"

The five adults stepped outside as the Texans pulled their mounts to a stop in front of them. Through the dust raised by their scrambling halt, Elliot caught sight of his horse being led by one of the cowboys. Angrily, he started for it, but the Texan who was holding the mount cantered closer to Elliot and flung the reins at him. Snatching at them, Elliot was about to say something, thought better of it, and led the recovered horse back toward the cabin.

The lead cowboy, the one who seemed to be in charge, touched the brim of his hat to Tom Bonwell. "Much obliged for the water, granger. Sorry if we trampled your crops some, but that grass'll spring right back up again soon's we get these cattle penned."

"No, it won't—not in time for harvesting," Tom shot back bitterly. "You've near ruined me!"

The trail boss was a lean fellow with a creased face, light blue eyes, and a thin smile that seemed somewhat contemptuous. "Well, who the hell do you think you are, anyway, sodbuster? Ripping up these grasslands and ruining them with your damned plows. I seen your kind before. You come in like locusts, tear up the grasses, go broke, and move on."

"That's not true!" Louise shouted, outraged.

"Beggin' your pardon, ma'am, but it surely is."

Wheeling his horse around, the Texan led his men

off in the direction of the barn. With a weak cry, Louise ran a few steps, watched, and then flung herself, sobbing, into her husband's arms.

"My garden!" she wailed. "My garden! They're riding right through it!"

Watching the riders go, Tom groaned. "There goes a summer's work—and this winter's vegetables."

He looked at Jud then. "I don't care how long it takes, Jud, but I'll stick it out now. You say you need candidates to run for the city council? Okay, try me! I'll run!"

Jud clasped the man's hand and shook it fervently. "Now you're talking, Tom," he cried excitedly, "and the association will give you all the support you need!"

The Bonwell farm was only the first of several Jud took Elliot and Connie to visit. By the time they had been to three others in the vicinity, the two reporters were silent with outrage. Jud and his wife had a fine supper for them, but Elliot and Connie were anxious to return to Abilene that night and wouldn't be persuaded to stay.

They both had columns they wanted very much to write.

AN OPEN LETTER
TO THE CITIZENS OF ABILENE

It is about time that the decent citizens of Abilene asked themselves what they want for their burgeoning young metropolis. Is it to be more houses of ill repute, more wide-open gaming establishments, more killings, more instances of public intoxication? If so, then all they have to do is simply continue to allow the Texans and their hirelings to run Abilene—with money the only morality.

But surely, this is not what the decent, law-abiding citizens of Abilene really want. Yet, if they do nothing to curb the cattle trade, if they allow the Texans to take over the town every summer and make it their playground, this is all that the citizenry of Abilene can expect for the foreseeable future.

Accordingly, the *Abilene Chronicle* would now like to go on record as supporting wholeheartedly Jud Powell and the Farmers' Protective Association in their determination to rid Abilene of the cattle trade. And in addition, we urge all Texans who may be contemplating the possibility of driving their cattle to Abilene in the future to seek another shipping point. We hope that all Texans in Abilene today will carry this firm resolve back with them to the cattlemen of their fair state.

What prompts this front-page comment is a visit this editor made to four farms outside Abilene in the company of Jud Powell. It was a sobering and saddening experience, so much so that I have asked Connie Witherspoon, the editor of the *Chronicle*'s ladies' page, who accompanied Jud Powell and me on this tour, to describe in her own words what we saw.

Before you turn to the ladies' page and read Miss Witherspoon's account of our melancholy encounter with these Texas drovers, I suggest you remember one pertinent fact. Throughout their mean ruination of all they came across, not one of these so-called knights of the plains made the slightest apology for their behavior. Indeed, they seemed eager, even anxious, to reveal to us the scathing contempt they felt for those of our brethren humble enough to labor behind the plow.

In closing, I suggest that our future lies not with those mounted horsemen who despoil our land once a season, but with those who abide here throughout the year and enrich our lives with the fruit of their toil.

Glancing up from his desk, Elliot was pleased to see Miles Kramer, who had just returned from Hays City. A copy of the *Chronicle* in his hand, he was hurrying toward his office with a wide grin on his face. The *Chronicle*'s publisher knocked once, then pushed open the door. Slumping down into the chair beside Elliot's desk, he slapped the newspaper down on the blotter and shook his head in admiration.

"Capital!" he cried.

"I assume you mean my front-page editorial."

He nodded vigorously. "And Connie's fine eyewitness account. Why, man, it reads like a novel!"

"I'm glad you liked it. How long have you been back?"

"Just got off the train and came right over. Everyone in town has his nose buried in the *Chronicle*!" He shook his head. "At first I thought there might have been another shooting."

"You don't think we went too far, do you?"

Miles emphatically shook his head from side to side. "It was well-nigh perfect. That was a fine stroke—letting Connie tell it from her point of view. And when she told about that farm wife's garden . . ." He shook his head angrily as he recalled the incident. "I am certain there is not a lady in Abilene who will not know what Mrs. Bonwell felt."

Elliot smiled. "Fine. I am writing another front-page editorial for the next issue. This time I am suggesting that the city council is going to have to listen to the farmers—not to the businessmen who get fat on the Texans."

"Good. I'll back you on that, certainly." He leaned back and laughed expansively. "I must admit, Elliot, once you get the bit in your teeth, you move right along. I don't mind admitting now that I was beginning to wonder if I had made a mistake in hiring you."

Elliot's eyebrows shot up a notch. "That so, Miles? How come?"

"Well, you remember what I told you the first day—I wanted the *Chronicle* to take sides on this debate. Until now you've been relatively quiet, content to give the Farmers' Protective Association free publicity without taking any public stance."

Elliot nodded. "Perhaps you are right, Miles. Perhaps I was going a bit too slowly. But after what I saw yesterday, I decided to pull out all the stops. This cattle trade must be diverted."

"Precisely." Miles looked shrewdly at Elliot. "You know, for a while there I was also beginning to think your friendship with Wild Bill Hickok was altering your perception of the problem."

"Wild Bill is a friend, Miles. I will not deny that. But you underestimate him if you think he does not understand as well as you and I how much of a curse this cattle trade has become for Abilene."

Glancing up, Elliot saw Connie approaching and got to his feet. As he hurried to open the door for her, he realized how anxious he was to hear Miles share with Connie his enthusiasm for their work on this story.

As a team, it seemed, they were doing just fine.

In a banquet room above the Alamo, a group of townsmen were gathered for a stag dinner. The three courses had been put away with great gusto, and those drinking were now on their second round. The air in the room was alive with thick coils of cigar smoke, and laughter was erupting from all corners as the newest ribald jokes were exchanged. There was much backslapping and general merriment all around—except when anyone had the audacity to bring up the front-page editorial in that afternoon's edition of the *Abilene Chronicle*. Controversial though it was, Elliot Carson and Miles Kramer were among those in attendance, and there was not a man in the room who did not make the two feel welcome.

Sitting at the head table between Abilene's founding fathers, Joe McCoy and T. C. Henry, Hickok fidgeted nervously. There was a yawning emptiness at his back as well as a window that looked out onto an alley. That they were on the third floor of the Alamo gave Hickok little comfort. To add to his unease, he had been aware of occasional sly glances from the dinner guests, and it began to dawn on him that he was the guest of honor. If so, the reason for him being singled out in this fashion escaped him completely.

T. C. Henry began rapping on his glass with his spoon, and at once the assembled guests quieted. This time—without any attempt to mask their curiosity—more than half the men looked with pleased amusement directly at Hickok.

The marshal's stomach sank. He was it—no doubt about it.

Getting up from his chair, T. C. Henry patted Hickok lightly on the shoulder, then moved over to the speaker's podium and took from his inside jacket pocket a small piece of paper, which he proceeded to unfold with elaborate gestures. Propping his glasses on his nose, he cleared his throat.

"Bill!" the man boomed, looking directly at the

marshal. "I suppose you've guessed by now that something's up."

The gentle laughter grew in volume as Hickok nodded unhappily, and then T. C. turned to address the guests.

"When Joe and I decided to transform this whistle-stop into a mecca for Texas steers, we never dreamed it would turn into the hell on wheels it did. But gentlemen, here we are! So drink up!"

There was appreciative laughter and a few whoops as glasses were lifted in toasts.

"But that's not why we are here tonight. No sir. We are not here to congratulate ourselves, or to decide which way this town is to go in the future. For now, Abilene and the Texas drovers who descend on it each summer are facts. Unpleasant facts for some . . ." T. C. glanced at Elliot and Miles, but there was no malice in the glance, only a sober awareness of what Elliot felt. ". . . But ones that we have to live with, at least for now. Of course, we all know we're sitting on a powder keg, but you can't please everyone, and life has to go on—even the life of our less respectable citizens."

There was a general mutter of assent to that.

"But we all know how difficult our lives here would be were it not for those who have the courage and steely backbone to walk these streets and place themselves between us and damnation. Not so long ago, that man—and dammit, you all know to whom I am referring—put himself on the line when he charged up a dark stairway and exchanged shots with a Texan who was firing on Joe Taylor. That Texan is still alive to regret his foolhardy action, but more to the point, Joe Taylor is alive today, too, and so is our great town marshal!"

He paused and smiled as the room erupted in applause. Hickok felt his face reddening.

"You deserve that applause, Bill," T. C. Henry went on as soon as the applause subsided. "But now we want to give you something a bit more tangible to show our regard and affection." T. C. looked at Elliot Carson, smiled warmly, and nodded. "I'll let your friend Elliot show you what we mean, Bill." Folding up his speech and putting it back into his pocket, he waited while Elliot left his seat and walked up to the podium.

Elliot appeared slightly nervous as he took the small package from his side pocket and cleared his throat. "Thanks, T. C. I truly appreciate the opportunity to join in this tribute." Clearing his throat again, he looked at Hickok and said, "Would you come up here, Bill?"

Hickok pushed his chair back and walked stiffly up to the podium. His mouth was dry, his hands shaking slightly. He would rather have been walking into a dark alley after a crazed Texan, he told himself ruefully. Fleetingly, then, he thought of Agnes and wished she could have been there with him—for moral support, if nothing else.

Elliot was opening a small, white, flat box. Hickok knew it was a pocket watch before he saw it—he caught the glint of gold on the engraved back. Elliot held up the watch for all to see, and appreciative applause delayed further speech.

"I am going to read the inscription, Bill," Elliot said at last, clearing his throat again.

Hickok was wondering why it was getting so difficult for him to swallow.

Elliot looked down at the watch as he said, "There's today's date, of course, and then the inscription reads, 'J. B. Hickok from his friends.'"

Elliot looked up then and smiled. The applause came softly at first, then grew to a tumultuous, thunderous wave. Someone in front stood up, still applauding, and everyone else was soon on his feet, some cheering, others stomping. The genuine warmth of this response overwhelmed Hickok. He felt his throat constricting painfully and wanted to run somewhere and hide. At the same time, he realized that this was the proudest moment of his life.

The ovation finally subsiding, Elliot stepped closer to Bill and handed him the watch. "Your friends want you to wear this in good health, Bill, and for many good years ahead."

Applause erupted a second time, then quieted quickly as everyone watched Hickok accept the gift and waited for him to speak. Carefully taking the gold timepiece from Elliot, Hickok tried to clear his throat to say something, but he simply could not get the words out. His vision blurred, and he blinked quickly to clear it. Then he looked around at all the smiling faces and tried again, only to give up and wave his hands in thanks. After shaking Elliot's hand, then T. C.'s, Abilene's marshal fled to his chair. As he sat down, Joe McCoy slapped him fondly on the back. Hickok nodded his thanks once again, then ducked his head, ostensibly to set and wind his new watch.

On the podium T. C. Henry thanked Elliot and declared it was time to bring on the girls. A roar greeted that suggestion, and Hickok was grateful for the opportunity to fade back into the wallpaper. His new watch now set to the correct time, he wound it and dropped it into his vest pocket.

First thing in the morning he would purchase a suitable chain and fob, then show it to Agnes, he told himself. She would be as pleased as he was. The thought of her shared pride warmed him as he leaned back in his chair to greet the steady stream of well-wishers now coming up to shake the hand of Wild Bill Hickok.

Chapter 8

The same night that Wild Bill was being feted in the Alamo, Ma Ruby brought Sue Ann down to meet a new customer: Jim Mulrey.

Gasping, Sue Ann pulled back, but Ma Ruby's iron fingers dug into her arm, preventing her from turning and bolting back up the stairs. Mulrey saw Sue Ann's reaction, but it did not appear to discourage him. In fact, Ruby thought the gleam in his eye appeared to brighten.

"Thanks, Ruby," he said with a lecherous sneer. "I know Sue Ann from way back. I been meaning to visit before this, but I been busy." He looked directly at Sue Ann and winked. "Hi, Sue. There'll be a big tip waitin' for you—and for Ruby here—when this night's through."

"You hear that, dearie?" Ruby said to Sue Ann. "Ain't that nice? Now you two go on upstairs and enjoy yourselves."

Frowning slightly, Ruby watched Mulrey take Sue Ann's hand as she went before him up the stairs. The last thing Ruby needed now was a temperamental girl—and this Sue Ann had been getting worse, not better, of late. Crying in her room at all hours . . . refusing certain customers . . . Well, the girl would not turn this one down—not if she wanted to stay at Ruby Winstead's house.

The trade had been off lately, and Ruby knew the cause. The Texans had taken a fancy to a new place a few blocks down—to the Mexican girls the black madam had imported. Ruby was outraged not only because they were taking away her business with foreign girls but because those Mexican girls were sometimes less than twelve years old. It was only with great difficulty that she was able to keep her indignation within bounds. She liked to have a few young girls in her house as well—but never would she allow a girl she knew was *that* young to work for her. That was going too far.

Sue Ann and Jim Mulrey disappeared up the stairs. Satisfied, Ma Ruby hurried back into the parlor to finish her game of whist.

Sitting on the edge of the bed, Sue Ann waited for Jim Mulrey to get undressed. After a while he straightened, naked except for the dirt that covered him, and reached out for her.

"Ma Ruby says you got to wash first," Sue Ann said, pointing to the washstand in the corner. She was relieved to have another moment before giving in to this vile man. He was the only man she knew who could make her feel soiled by just looking at her.

"Aw, hell. Forget what Ruby says."

"I daren't. She'll let me go if I don't insist."

"You take off that shift, then."

"Do I have to?"

"Yes, you do. I want to see you." His eyes gleamed in the dim room, and then he smiled. "I want to see all of you . . . like the girls do in New Orleans."

"Well, this isn't New Orleans."

Suddenly he reached out and ripped her smock down the front, then tossed it aside. Sue Ann cringed away from him. He laughed without sympathy, grabbed her wrists, and bore her down underneath him.

"Not . . . until . . . you . . . *wash*," Sue Ann said between gritted teeth as she kept her face averted from his.

"Oh, shit!" Mulrey exploded, standing up and walking to the washstand, where he quickly rinsed his hands. When he returned to Sue Ann, she rolled away, and the rank-smelling man angrily reached out and grabbed her hair, then yanked her back. Sue Ann cried out in pain.

"I'm payin' for you, so you better lay still!"

"I don't want to. I'm . . . sick!"

He pulled back quickly. "What do you mean? You got something?"

Sue Ann took a deep breath. If she told Mulrey she had a disease, she would be out of the house that night, walking the streets once more, being grabbed and used by worse men than Ma Ruby's clients—and for nothing. She shook her head miserably.

"I just said that so I could get my breath. If you weren't so rough, it wouldn't be so bad for me."

He smiled. "I won't be rough—I promise. But you got to be nice to me. *Real* nice."

A new tone in his voice alerted her that Mulrey had something out of the ordinary in mind. She looked at him closely. "What do you mean?"

"I'm payin' double to keep you all night." Mulrey grinned. "So we got time to try lots of things."

"What kinds of things?" she cried, panic flooding her.

Quickly, he reached out and rolled her over onto her stomach.

"Now, just lie easy. It might hurt a little at first, but you'll see how nice it is."

Confused, Sue Ann tried to turn her head. *What*

123

was he doing? Then she felt him . . . and at first she thought he had made a mistake. Then she realized he was serious. She tried to roll over, but he was too strong for her and lunged at her with greater force. The pain was so intense she could hardly believe it. She screamed . . . and kept on screaming.

Slapping at her and cursing her, Mulrey rolled away just as the door opened and Ruby burst into the room. Ignoring Mulrey completely, Ruby glared down at Sue Ann.

"You stop that screaming this instant!" she cried. "What's the matter with you? You'll be out in the streets tonight if you don't shut up!"

Through great, racking sobs Sue Ann told Ruby what Jim had been doing, but to her horror, Ruby seemed not in the least disturbed by her account. Instead, Ma Ruby seemed to be getting angry with *her!*

Ruby turned to Mulrey. "I'm sorry, Jim. I guess Sue Ann's not feeling too well this evening. But you did ask for her, and I didn't want to disappoint you." She smiled as she led him toward the door. "Have you met Angelique? I think she would be more than glad to cater to your fancies. She is a very interesting girl."

Jim looked regretfully back at Sue Ann, then shrugged. "All right," he said. "Let me get my things."

"No need," Ruby said quickly. "I'll get them. You go on into the next room, and I'll get Angelique."

As Mulrey left the room, Ruby gathered up his things. Turning to Sue Ann, she hissed, "I'll tend to you later!" She then swept out of the tiny room and pulled the door shut firmly behind her.

Choking on her sobs, Sue Ann dressed hurriedly, waited at the door for Angelique to join Mulrey in the next room, and then fled down the stairs and out of the house, heading for the Alamo . . . on the chance she might find Mike Williams there.

It was close to one o'clock in the morning. The testimonial dinner was over, and the citizens of Abilene had returned to the comfort and security of their homes. Hickok, though, had returned to his usual table along the wall in the Alamo.

Mike had been there waiting for him, the three other deputies already having retired to their night's lodgings. Hickok proudly showed his newest deputy the watch that had been presented to him earlier at the banquet. Hefting it, then reading the inscription, Mike grinned and handed it back to Hickok.

"That's a fine watch, Bill," he said. "Must've been some party up there."

"Sure was. Looks like a quiet night down here, though," Hickok remarked, glancing around at the nearly empty Alamo.

The six-man orchestra was playing with little enthusiasm, and behind the bar, the two barkeeps were trying to keep busy by polishing glasses. Hickok could not remember having seen the glasses stacked that high or gleaming with such splendor. The craps and faro tables were both empty; the roulette wheel, silent.

Hickok began to shuffle a deck of cards. He hated to admit it, but he missed Jess. With her absent from the Alamo—and no longer sharing Hickok's table—there was a noticeable dearth of eager poker players, especially the high rollers Jess usually attracted. He missed her for other reasons, too.

Hickok took out his new watch again. Turning it over and over in his hand, he inspected its workmanship. The face was particularly handsome, with its myriad of fine lines tracing an intricate design along the rim. The hands were clean and bright, the numbers clear. The casing was evidently solid gold.

"Yes sir, Bill," Mike said, as he looked over at the timepiece. "That watch shows they really appreciate you in this town."

Hickok nodded. "Guess maybe it does at that." He slipped the watch quickly into his vest pocket, slightly embarrassed that Mike had caught him examining his gift.

The handsome timepiece must have cost nearly a month's wages, and despite his pleasure at the honor, Hickok found himself wondering if perhaps it might not have been a better idea for them to have given him a raise. He did well enough at poker, but one hundred and fifty dollars a month plus twenty-five percent of all fines imposed in court did not go very far in a high-tariff trail town where nothing could be bought for less than twenty-five cents. Two bits was the cost of a drink or a shave, with everything else priced higher in proportion.

"Two more trail herds on the way," Mike remarked idly, sipping his beer. "I just heard."

"I don't know whether to cheer or whimper," said Hickok, pulling his rye toward him.

"Hey, Mike! . . ."

Mike turned and saw Butterfield. The big bartender indicated the rear of the Alamo with a toss of his head. Hickok, peering into the gloom, made out the figure of a girl huddled by the back door.

"Sue Ann!" Mike cried, jumping to his feet.

Hickok watched as Mike hurried over to the girl, stooping down to comfort her. Sue Ann's head dropped forward onto Mike's chest, and Hickok saw her frail shoulders shudder as she tried to explain the reason for her present state. The sound of her sobbing frequently interrupted her story. After she had quieted somewhat,

Mike led the unhappy girl over to Hickok's table and held the chair for her as she sat down. She nodded gratefully when Mike offered to get her a drink.

As Mike walked up to the bar, Hickok smiled at the distraught girl in an effort to put her at ease. The smile she returned was tentative, even fearful, and Hickok could not help but compare her present beaten attitude with her former undauntable assurance. Sue Ann was now an unhappy sinner, pitiful in her misery. Though Hickok had foreseen this inevitable turn in her fortunes, witnessing it coming to pass saddened him.

Mike returned with her drink, a watered-down glass of scotch, and set it down in front of her. Sue Ann drank it in one desperate gulp.

"I don't have anyplace to go, Mike," she said, her voice close to breaking.

"Sure you do—my place. There's no need for you ever to go back to Ma Ruby's, Sue Ann. I promise."

Tears streaming down her sallow cheeks, Sue Ann reached out and took Mike's hand in gratitude and squeezed it. Mike turned to Hickok.

"That damn Jim Mulrey! This is all his fault. Sue Ann didn't want to go with him, but Ruby made her. That man's an animal!"

Hickok wanted to sympathize but couldn't. "Well, now, Mike," he said, shrugging helplessly. "As long as Jim paid the going price . . ."

Sue Ann winced. Mike's face reddened, but he said nothing. He knew only too well that Hickok spoke the truth.

"Come on," Mike told Sue Ann. "I'm taking you to my place. You need a good night's rest. It will all look better in the morning, just you wait and see."

Nodding wearily, Sue Ann got to her feet and allowed Mike to lead her from the Alamo.

Watching them go, Hickok sighed and finished his

drink. It would do no good for him to warn Mike; to warn anyone about a member of the opposite sex was at best an exercise in futility. Getting up from the table, he stretched wearily, waved to Butterfield, and left the Alamo. Moving swiftly, warily down the middle of the empty street, he reached the Drovers' Cottage and was pleased to find Agnes waiting up for him in the lobby, a book in her lap.

As he approached her, she dropped a bookmark on the page she was reading and closed the book. He settled into an easy chair beside her.

"Kind of late, even for you, ain't it, Agnes?"

"I cannot tell a lie. I was waiting for you. I heard about the testimonial dinner, James, and I am so proud. May I see the watch?"

"If you hadn't asked, I would have shown it to you anyway," he said, pulling it out. "I've been wearing it out just looking at it."

She took it from him and inspected it carefully. "It is such a fine watch, James . . . and I do like the inscription." She smiled at him. "You see, you do have many friends in Abilene, people who appreciate what you are doing."

"It's good to know," Hickok replied, nodding. Then he smiled. "Still, I would have preferred a raise."

"A raise you would spend and forget. This watch you will keep with you forever, James. Whenever you consult it, you will think of this town and the men who thought enough of you to present you with it."

As Hickok took the watch back from her, he smiled. "And I will think of you, as well, Agnes . . . waiting here for me and telling me this."

He got up, and Agnes rose with him.

"Good night, Agnes. Thanks for waiting up for me. If I had known, I would have left the Alamo sooner."

"Good night, James." They smiled warmly at each other for a long moment, and then Agnes turned toward the stairs.

Hickok was still thinking of Agnes Thatcher as he made ready for bed, deeply touched by her patient vigil in the lobby. A strange woman, indeed, Agnes was. She seemed convinced she loved him, yet it did not make her overly persistent; in fact, she did not ask anything of him in return. All she wanted was for him to be well and happy—at least, that was how it appeared.

While he was occupied with these thoughts, Hickok was busy tending to his nightly task of crumpling up pages of newspapers and strewing them around his bed and near the window and door. Anyone who entered the room during the night would unwittingly trigger this simple alarm and with the first step waken the marshal. Hickok had learned long ago that truly restful sleep was impossible for him without such precaution. Finished, he turned down the lamp and got into his bed. He was exhausted, physically and emotionally. Fitting his right hand over the grip of the Navy Colt tucked under his pillow, he closed his eyes. His last image as he drifted off was of the steady stream of smiling townsmen coming up to shake his hand. . . .

A foot disturbed the crumpled newspaper near the door.

Hickok was awake instantly, a cold sweat breaking out on his forehead. His hand closed tightly around the Colt's grip, and just then more newspaper was stepped on, this time much closer to the bed. Waiting an instant longer, Hickok flung around, shoving the muzzle of his revolver into the belly of his startled would-be assassin.

Jess's shocked cry almost caused Hickok to drop his weapon.

"Jess! What in hell are you up to!" he demanded hoarsely, leaning back onto the bed, the revolver dangling from his hand. "I almost blew your belly open."

"You gave me your key, Bill. Don't you remember?"

He looked at her in the dim light and shook his head wearily. "Hell, I thought you'd lost it."

"I know," she said, stepping closer to him and dropping down onto the edge of the bed. "It's been a long time."

"It sure as hell has, Jess—too damn long. So why the sudden interest?"

"I've been a fool, Bill. If you hadn't run off on me like that in front of the Bull's Head, I would have admitted it then."

"That was a fine place to discuss things—in front of the Bull's Head, with half the town watching. Jess, if you wanted to tell me anything, you knew where to find me. For the past couple of weeks, Kelly's been asking what happened to you. I finally had to tell him to back off."

"You knew where to find me, Bill. So did Kelly."

"Sure, in the Bull's Head—where your friends Coe and Thompson stood up to me and gave Mulrey his alibi. You know damn well he was the one who shot at me that night. Jess, with friends like you, I don't need enemies."

"Shut up," she said softly, fiercely. "I told you, I made a mistake. Now let me make it up to you."

As she spoke, she bent closer. Her lips opened his and her tongue darted with unsettling wantonness into his mouth. As her fingers swiftly unbuttoned the front of her dress, she pushed him gently back, her lips still fastened to his. He let his weapon drop to the floor as he pulled her closer.

In a moment, with an expertise that never ceased

to amaze him, she was completely naked beside him, and he had already forgotten what it was they had been arguing about.

Feeling more alive than he had in a long time, Hickok lit the lamp and scooted up in his bed so that his back rested against the brass rails at its head. As soon as he was comfortable, he pulled Jess up against him, her cheek resting against his chest. She snuggled close, contented, as he stroked her red curls.

"Now tell me," he said to Jess. "How come this sudden change of heart?"

"Well, you did tell me you and Agnes were just friends. Of course, I didn't believe you. After all—as you must know, you big, curly-headed bastard—that woman is head over heels in love with you."

"There's nothing I can do about that," he told her, grinning. "Of course, I can understand how she feels."

Jess dug her elbow in his side, and he winced playfully.

"Anyway, if you must know," Jess went on, "I heard about the testimonial dinner, and I wanted to congratulate you, so I was waiting downstairs in the lobby for you. When I saw you go right over to Agnes, I was ready to march right out. . . ." She snuggled closer to him. "And then I saw how you were with her. When you said good night to her and went up to your room alone, I knew what a fool I had been."

"You want to repeat that again?"

Jess nudged him again and then laughed. "I *was* a fool."

"Well, I can't argue with anything you've said so far, I must admit."

Again she jabbed him in his side with her elbow. "As soon as you went upstairs, I left the lobby and went to my room to get the key you gave me." She lifted her face to his and kissed him on the lips. "And here I am."

"So what's next, Jess?"

"That's up to you, Bill."

"Despite this testimonial dinner, Jess, I got the feeling that Abilene is getting ready to say good-bye to me."

"But why?"

"You read that editorial on the *Chronicle*'s front page today, didn't you? Abilene's days as a trail town are numbered. The farmers will be taking over soon."

"Hell, Bill, if that happens, we'll both have to pack our bags."

"Just what I was thinking. Of course, there'll be other trail towns down the line. . . ."

"Is that what you want for yourself, Bill?"

Hickok took a deep breath. "No," he said. "Still, I don't see what choice I have. These two guns and a deck of cards are the only equipment I got for making a living. You got any better idea?"

"I sure have!" Jess sat up and looked at him. "Do like Buffalo Bill's doing—go east and get on the stage!"

"You must be crazy. What would I do on the stage? I am no actor!"

"You don't have to be an actor. Just be yourself, Bill. Don't you see? You're famous! People would pay just to look at you. You could tell them about the hundred men you shot . . . and your days as a Pony Express rider and your gunfights."

"You say Buffalo Bill's doing that?"

"Why, he's even gone to England to visit the queen. Hell, I'll bet you shot as many buffalo as he did."

"I shot quite a few, but not as many as Buffalo Bill Cody."

"That doesn't matter. You're just as famous."

132

"Maybe you should be my manager," he said, laughing.

"Exactly what I had in mind." She snuggled against him again.

"Well, right now," Hickok told her, "I got something else on my mind." He leaned over and closed her mouth with his own. For only a moment did she try to protest, and then she flung her arms around his neck, pulling him down upon her.

Sue Ann could not sleep. She looked down at Mike, who lay on the floor beside the bed, wrapped in a blanket, his head resting on one arm. The sound of his gentle snoring was not what was keeping her awake, however.

Before Mike had tucked her in, he had insisted that she was going to be all right now, that her days of working in Ma Ruby's whorehouse were behind her. But as eager as she was to believe him, Sue Ann knew he was wrong.

Softly, stealthily, so as not to awaken Mike, she got out of bed and crept to the window. Over the roofs she could see the moon riding low in the sky. The night was beautiful; yet it made her shudder. She could not forget that it was during the night when the men came to her—big men, old men, small men, lean men. All through the night they came . . . and only with dawn was her odious labor done. Then came blessed, oblivious sleep, then a piece of the day, a drink or two to fortify her, and once more—all too soon—the long night would begin again.

At first it had been an exciting adventure. She had begun to feel desire and even passion stirring within her—despite her wish not to let it happen. Then the men Ruby sent to her began changing. Sue Ann realized what Ruby had done. The first johns the madam had selected for her newest girl were relatively attractive and inexperienced. Most of them were young cowboys up from Texas on their first trail drive. Some were even younger than Sue Ann, while the rest were her age or only a few years older.

Only when Sue Ann had proven her capability did Ruby send to her the older men who so craved her youth and freshness; from then on, with hardly an exception, the men who went upstairs with her were brutish and crass, with hard, callused hands, teeth decaying in their skulls, and their clothing rotting on their dirt-encrusted bodies. It was when these filthy creatures began accompanying Sue Ann up the stairs that she got a clear look at the pit into which she had fallen.

There was one bent-over old man she would never forget, not as long as she lived. He had sat on the edge of the bed, his head down and his face averted, while he explained to her what he wanted. At first she had listened incredulously, sure it was some kind of ugly joke, but then she realized the old man was serious! Recalling that twisted man reminded Sue Ann of her father. She shuddered.

Sue Ann had really run away from home because of her pap. He had alternately beat her and fondled her, and a few weeks before she had finally left for good, Pap had almost succeeded in raping her. When she had fought him off successfully, she had been proud of her resistance. Nevertheless, he had called her a whore, had railed at her viciously, insisting that it was all her fault for leading him on.

Now, as she stood by the window and thought of these past terrible weeks, she wondered if Pap hadn't been right, after all. Bowing her face in her hands, she tried to stifle a sob. Hugging herself, she turned and stumbled back to the bed, hauling the covers quickly up over her shoulders.

"Sue Ann? . . ."

It was Mike standing beside the bed, anxiously peering down at her.

"Go back to sleep," she told him, scrunching down still farther into the bed.

He sat next to her on the bed, stroking her hair as he pleaded, "Don't cry, Sue Ann. I hate it when you cry. Try to think of what's to come. We'll get married . . . I promise!"

"No!" Her sobs intensified.

"Yes!" He took her gently by the shoulder and rolled her over to face him. Kissing away her tears, he repeated his promise to her and told her once again that she was free of Ma Ruby now and that from this day on he would take care of her.

Sue Ann finally gave up trying to reason with him, agreeing to everything he told her just so that he would go back to sleep. As she listened to him breathing on the floor beside her, she stared up at the ceiling, searching over and over in her mind for a solution to her dilemma.

If she were to allow Mike to marry her, she was sure their life together wouldn't last. How would he ever be able to trust her? And there would come the day when the truth about her past would track them down, ruining whatever life they tried to build together.

It was too late for her now—she would only make matters worse by marrying Mike. She had already ruined one life; it would be a sin even Jesus could not forgive if she ruined Mike's life as well.

Eyes open, she lay back and stared up at the ceiling throughout the rest of the night. As the first faint rays of the new day filtered into the room, Sue Ann closed her eyes. She could sleep at last. She knew what she had to do.

Chapter 9

Agnes Lake Thatcher was on her way to the hotel dining room for breakfast when she heard a bright, melodious peal of laughter behind her. Looking back, she saw James coming down the stairs with a red-haired woman, whose arm was linked in his. One glance told Agnes all she needed to know: James and the redhead had spent the night together. The animal contentment both exuded made this conclusion inevitable.

Agnes turned and continued on into the dining room, heading for her favorite table. Neither James nor the girl had seen her, and for that she was grateful. The redheaded girl was very pretty—in a bold, brassy way—and much younger than James. Why James would want to make love to her instead of to a woman five years older than he was obvious . . . men would always prefer younger women. It was the way of the world.

Still, she had hoped against hope that other factors would gradually shift the balance in her favor, and for a while she had almost felt that her patient willingness to remain at his side without becoming a nuisance had done much to close the gap between them. Indeed, last night he had seemed truly grateful to find her waiting for him. The pleasure he had taken in showing her the watch had filled her with warmth, and for just a moment they had seemed to be so close. . . .

She sat down at her table and reached for the menu. The tears in her eyes made it impossible for her to read it, but she knew it by heart now anyway, so her blurred vision did not matter. She told herself she was acting foolishly, that she had no right to feel like this. What James wanted for himself—happiness and contentment—was what she wanted for him. He had never pretended there was anything more than friendship between them. If James was happy with this girl, then Agnes had no choice but to be happy for him.

But somehow she could not manage this. She felt miserable, utterly and completely devastated, as she continued to stare blindly down at the menu, allowing the tears to track their way down her freshly rouged cheeks.

"Pardon me, Mrs. Thatcher . . ."

Startled, Agnes looked up to see Major Farber standing beside her table, a hesitant smile on his face. His Vandyke beard was neatly trimmed, and the rest of his face was scrubbed to an almost cherubic shine. Even his glowing nose appeared somewhat subdued— the man had obviously applied talcum to it. Dressed in a fresh, neatly pressed white linen suit, the major exuded an air of confident prosperity. The moment his eyes caught Agnes Thatcher's, his smile broadened.

"Please forgive me for intruding," he said, doffing his hat, "but I took a room at this fine hostelry only last night and could not help but notice you sitting alone in the lobby for most of the evening . . . and now I see you at your breakfast, still alone. Since we met on the stagecoach, Mrs. Thatcher, I was hoping you would not consider me impertinent if I joined you for breakfast."

By the end of this formidable speech, Agnes found her eyes were almost dry. With a quick, pleased laugh, she said, "Why, sit right down, Major. It is truly a pleasure to see you again!"

The two were soon engaged in eager conversation as their breakfast became no longer a solitary, functional meal, but an opportunity for a pleasant chat.

Mike Williams spied Wild Bill as the marshal was saying good-bye to Jess Hazell. Across the street, the two were standing close together on the steps leading into one of the nicer rooming houses in Abilene. As soon as the marshal left Jess, Mike crossed the street and overtook him.

Turning to look down at the deputy, who was falling into step beside him, Hickok smiled. "Morning, Mike. How's Sue Ann?"

"That's what I wanted to tell you," Mike said happily. "Sue's going to settle down—she promised. I spoke to her last night about leaving Ma Ruby's and then again this morning. She's real quiet, Bill, but she's decided to stay with me."

Frowning, Hickok turned into a small restaurant he favored. The two men found a table against a wall to the rear of the place and sat down.

As soon as they had ordered, Hickok looked closely at Mike.

"You thinking of marrying that girl?" he asked, frowning again.

"I know it sounds crazy," Mike replied, "but that's just what I am planning. 'Course Sue Ann's going to shy away from that kind of talk at first—her head is full of nonsense about her being no good for me, since she's been working in that place—but I'll convince her soon enough."

"You're that confident, are you?"

"I love her, Bill. It's as simple as that."

"There isn't anything simple about love, Mike . . . but I guess you'll have to find that out for yourself."

"Don't you like Sue Ann, Bill?"

"Hell, I don't even know the girl. It isn't that, Mike . . . it's what I just told you. There's nothing simple or easy about a man and woman coming together. But of course, we don't usually find that out till later."

"When it's too late, you mean."

"That's what I mean."

Mike shrugged and looked at Hickok with unfazed happiness. "Don't you worry about me, Bill. I'm going to make Sue Ann happy . . . I'm going to take good care of her. Just you see."

Hickok smiled, bowing before the young man's youthful optimism. And what the hell—no one would ever make a cent selling caution to a man in love.

When their breakfast arrived, Mike ordered coffee and sandwiches—which he planned to take up to Sue Ann as soon as he finished his breakfast, he explained to Hickok.

"If you marry Sue Ann, are you going to stay in Abilene?" Hickok asked.

"Probably not. Think maybe I'll go back to Omaha with her. That's her hometown."

"I was hoping you'd say that," the marshal replied. "This trail town is on its last legs, I'm afraid." He smiled at Mike. "And I'll bet you've just about had it yourself as deputy. Am I right?"

Ruefully, Mike nodded. "You're right, Bill. I've had a bellyful of drunks stinking of their own vomit and cowboys carrying guns bigger than their brains."

"You mean you're sick of the glory?"

"Glory? . . . What glory, Bill?"

"Exactly," Hickok said, reaching for his coffee.

*　　*　　*

Sue Ann stirred fitfully, then opened her eyes. The morning sun was almost too much for her, and she looked away from it, throwing off the bedclothes. She realized she was wearing one of Mike's shirts—and nothing else—but she paid little heed to this as she attended to her toilet, then slumped back down on the bed, trying to rub the sleep out of her eyes.

The events of the night before came back to her, filling her with a crawling horror the instant she remembered Jim Mulrey. For just a moment she wished that Mike had not left her, that he had remained here beside her. She needed his optimism now, his eagerness to put her terrible sinfulness behind them. . . .

But he was not here. And in her twisted perspective she decided she was glad for that. Mike would only attempt to stop her from doing what she must. There was no help for it, no turning back. Her soul was damned through all eternity, just as Pap had said. Everything she had done since running away was only a confirmation of her ugly wickedness.

Sue Ann remembered hearing Mike whisper in her ear before he left. He said he would bring back her breakfast and that she should stay in bed and sleep. *How long has he been gone?* she wondered dully. But that didn't matter—not if she acted swiftly.

Pushing herself off the bed, she walked over to the top of Mike's dresser. What she was looking for was right on the top of it, next to his shaving brush. Opening the straight razor, she deftly ran her forefinger over the blade . . . and the blood came almost unbidden. Yes, it was sharp enough.

She returned to the bed and drew the covers over her shoulders. The morning sun poured into the room with such intensity that she could not concentrate on her task. In one swift movement, she jumped from the bed, pulled the shades all the way down, and then crawled back under the blankets.

Yes, that was much better. Taking a firm grip on the handle of the straight razor, she rested the blade against the underside of her wrist. Then, gently, but with firm determination, she leaned her weight forward until she felt the sharp, electric bite of the razor's edge. It was not so bad, not nearly so bad as she had expected. She kept her full weight on her burning wrist, and after a moment or two, she felt a warm wetness beneath her as the mattress greedily feasted on her blood, soaking it up. A curious, almost drunken lightheadedness fell over her, and for just a moment she wondered if she were making a mistake. But it was too late now for such questions, she realized almost gratefully . . . too late.

Her eyelids became leaden. Panic plucked at her for just an instant, then passed on. She sighed deeply, closed her eyes, and drifted off. . . .

Carrying Sue Ann's egg sandwiches and coffee into his room on a wooden tray, Mike scowled at the darkness, placed the tray on the top of his dresser, and then tiptoed over to the bed.

Sue Ann was burrowed face down in the pillow, her tousled curls barely visible under the covers. So soundly was she sleeping that Mike was reluctant to disturb her. After what she had been through, she needed all the sleep she could get. But the coffee and sandwiches would soon be cold, and nothing was worse than a cold egg sandwich, he told himself as he reached down and gently nudged her shoulder. When Sue Ann did not respond, he bent closer and kissed her on the back of the neck.

Straightening, he frowned slightly. Against his lips, her neck had felt like a block of stone. And she was still, so still . . . and it frightened him.

141

"*Sue Ann!*" he called to her.

There was no answer, no movement at all. Mike's knees went weak, and he faltered back. He was preparing to call out once more when he saw the dark, widening pool of blood beneath the bed.

Squinting in the pitiless light of midday, Connie Witherspoon watched the cheap pine box being lowered into the ground. It moved jerkily, caught for a moment along the side of the grave, and then dropped out of sight. Her tears obscuring the scene, Connie turned her face away. Beside her, Elliot put his arm around her shoulders and hugged her gently. Connie, surprised at the comfort his nearness gave her, rested her head against his shoulder.

Young Mike Williams bent numbly, grabbed a fistful of dirt, and listlessly cast it down onto the coffin. Hearing it drop onto the pine cover, he stood back. The preacher said a few more words, closed his prayer book, and nodded to the gravediggers, who then stepped forward casually and began shoveling dirt down onto the coffin.

The small party of mourners broke up and headed back through the graveyard toward their waiting buggies. Hickok stayed close to Mike, with Connie and Elliot just behind them. When Mike reached the buggy he and Hickok had rented, the marshal left his wan deputy and settled up with the preacher and the driver of the hearse. Connie stepped close to Mike then, and reaching out, she took his hand and squeezed it, saying nothing.

Mike looked at her blankly, as if unable to comprehend what had happened. Returning at that moment, Hickok nodded to her, climbed in beside Mike, and slapped the reins. The buggy spurted forward.

Elliot moved up beside Connie as the buggy rattled down the road. "If I am any judge," he said, "Hickok will get Mike drunk as a lord. The trouble is, in his condition that poor young man won't know the difference."

Connie shook her head in wonderment. "He certainly is taking it hard."

"Yes, he is."

"And all during that long stagecoach ride, the two of them hardly exchanged a word. Remember?"

"I remember," Elliot said, helping Connie up into the buggy. "I also remember he couldn't keep his eyes off her." Climbing up beside Connie, Elliot looked at her somberly. "Love is a strange thing. There's no rhyme or reason to it . . . or haven't you noticed?"

She looked quickly away from his searching eyes. "I've noticed."

Elliot took up the reins and followed Hickok back into Abilene.

When Connie and Elliot reached the *Chronicle* office, Miles Kramer was waiting for them outside. Opening the door for them, he pulled his editors eagerly inside.

"Get in here, you two," he said, leading them toward Elliot's office. "I've got something for your front page that's going to raise quite a ruckus."

Once inside his office, Elliot skirted his desk and slumped wearily down into his chair.

"Slow down, will you, Miles?" Elliot said wearily. "Connie and I have just come from a funeral. We both knew the girl—Sue Ann Mobley. She arrived in Abilene on the same stagecoach we were on—a bright, eager, innocent young girl. It didn't take long for Abilene to destroy her."

"Oh, yes," Miles said. "I heard about that. A suicide, wasn't it? Terrible thing . . . just terrible."

"I am going to write a column about it, Miles," Connie said.

"Fine . . . you do that." The publisher smiled at Connie. "You are beginning to get quite a following among the womenfolk of this town, young lady. I knew I had a capital idea when I suggested you take over the ladies' page."

"Connie is much more than the editor of the ladies' page, Miles," Elliot told him. "She is quite capable of handling any assignment we would care to give her. Whatever she has to say about Sue Ann's death will go on the front page. The trail-town mentality that brought such tragedy to pass is not back-page news, as far as I am concerned." He glanced up at Connie. "Is that what you had in mind, Connie?"

Pleased, she nodded. "Yes, Elliot. It is."

"Then go to it. We have enough time, I think, to get it into today's edition."

As Connie hurried from his office, Elliot looked up at Miles. "Now, Miles, just what is this news you have for me?"

"I just came from the town council. They've passed an ordinance that I am sure will do much to control the violence in this town. At any rate, it will certainly cause controversy."

At once Elliot was interested. He leaned forward. "You mean they've finally passed a law prohibiting the carrying of firearms within the limits of Abilene?"

"It's not that sweeping, Elliot. Here. Read it for yourself." Miles took from his inside pocket a rough draft of the new law and handed it to Elliot.

Elliot leaned back in his chair and read the ordinance. Though it did not ban the possession of firearms, the new law did ban the discharging of any pistol, revolver, or gun of any kind within the town limits of Abilene—in any street, alley, highway, lot, house, or other place where the life or limb of anyone could be endangered. Any person or persons who violated this ordinance would be punished by a fine of not less than ten dollars or more than one hundred dollars.

Glancing up at Miles, Elliot asked, "When does this take effect?"

"Tomorrow. But the council would like it to be on the front page today, if possible."

"Consider it done."

Rapping on the glass, Elliot caught the attention of Sam Burgmeister's apprentice. The fellow came running, and as soon as he opened the door, Elliot handed him the ordinance and told him he wanted it on that day's front page.

Closing the door, Elliot looked back at the publisher. "I must admit, Miles, if Bill can make this ordinance stick, it will be a great help. We all know how unnerving it is to hear the rattle of gunfire in this town, especially in the wee hours of the morning."

"Make no mistake, Elliot. We are under no delusion that this ordinance will be an easy one to enforce. In fact, doing so will more than likely stir up a hornet's nest."

"Then why pass it?"

"Elliot, for too long now we've handled this problem of firearms by ignoring it. I pushed this through the council because I think it is time we brought things to a head."

"It will do that, I am sure." Elliot said, frowning thoughtfully. "But I sure as hell wouldn't want to be in Wild Bill's shoes."

"Hell! If he's as tough as people say he is, this will be his opportunity to prove it. We've given him the tool he needs—an ordinance that will enable him to put a proper curb on these damn Texans."

Elliot nodded. It was time they faced up to this

145

insane, juvenile use of firearms. Liquored-up cowpokes fired off their revolvers at the slightest provocation, and many times for no reason at all—just sheer, animal high spirits. Elliot found himself recalling his first day in town, when he had rushed out to rescue Connie in the middle of Texas Street. Miles was absolutely right. If this ordinance could put a stop to such mindless behavior, it would be worth whatever trouble it might cause.

"Another thing, Elliot," Miles said, heading for the door. "It would help if you would compose an editorial calling attention to this ordinance. I want Abilene's citizens to know the *Chronicle* is fully behind it."

The door opened, and Miles stepped out of the way to let Connie enter. She had a sheet of paper in her hand, and she obviously wanted Elliot to see what she had written. Sensing this, Miles bid them good-bye and left.

As soon as the publisher was gone, Connie handed Elliot the paper. It was, as he had expected, Connie's column concerning the short, pathetic career of Sue Ann Mobley.

He read it quickly and was impressed. With a curt nod, he handed it back to her.

"Did you like it?" Connie asked.

"It is strong, unsentimental, and angry. I would not change a word. Now get out of here. I've got an editorial to write."

She stood for a moment, studying him, then leaned over impulsively and planted a light kiss on his forehead. Before he could react, she was gone, and he was left sitting in his chair, glowing. . . .

More and more, it seemed, they were finding themselves in perfect agreement.

Chapter 10

The *Abilene Chronicle* carried the new ordinance on its front page the same day that Sue Ann Mobley was buried. On the editorial page inside, Elliot left no doubt in anyone's mind how enthusiastic the *Chronicle* was in its support of this new town ordinance. Summing up his editorial, Elliot hailed the new law as "an attempt to restore order and sanity at last to the streets of Abilene."

Also on the front page was Connie's simple, unadorned account of Sue Ann Mobley's tragic death, one more reminder—if such were needed—of Abilene's sorry plight.

That night the town simmered. Hickok prowled the streets and saloons in the company of his deputies, on watch for violators, but they found none. Not a single six-gun was discharged during that long, tense night.

Early the next morning, however, word spread rapidly that the Texan whom Wild Bill had wounded in the Bull's Head a little more than two weeks before had died during the night, his hands still clutching his quivering, stinking vitals. His death came as a relief to the four Texans who had loyally tended him. Released from their grisly deathwatch, they proceeded to drown their frustration and sorrow in booze.

Around three that afternoon, the first of two rumored trail herds approached the outskirts of town. The cattle buyers swarmed out to meet it, and not long after, the herd's trail-weary cowboys hit town. Hickok and his deputies moved swiftly, hammering up the new ordinance on every wall and fence that could take a pounding. In addition, they visited the saloons and gambling halls to remind the incoming Texans of the new law.

There was not a single cowpoke who did not nod sagely when informed of the new law, admitting it was a good idea—a *damn* good idea, in fact. But that was in the afternoon, before any of them had yet had a chance to begin their annual attempt to drink the town dry and bay at the moon. Hickok took pains to remind his deputies of that.

The second trail herd arrived at four. Soon business in Abilene was better than it had been in weeks, and before the sun went down, a cowboy burst from the Pearl saloon, discharged his pistol into the sky, followed it with a whoop, then leaped on his horse and galloped down Texas Street, his bottle of whiskey brandished high.

Rushing from the Alamo, Hickok watched as the cowboy disappeared across the tracks. Taking a deep breath, he decided against going after the culprit, turned, and went back into the Alamo for what he presumed would be his last hand of the evening. It was going to be a long night.

Inside the Pearl, a saloon across from the depot, Major Farber was playing poker. He had been at this game table for the past two hours and was no longer the expansive gambler he had been when he first entered the saloon. The major had prevailed upon Agnes to accompany him—to bring him luck, as he had put

148

it—but for the last hour, sitting at a table to one side of the game, Agnes had watched as the pile of chips in front of him gradually melted away . . . like the spring snows. The cigar the major had been puffing on when the game began was now dead in his mouth, and beads of sweat were standing out on his forehead so clearly that even from her vantage point Agnes could see them as they gleamed through the heavy coils of blue smoke twisting in the air over the table. She had not brought the major luck at all, she realized.

Abruptly, Major Farber put his hand down and swore mildly. The thin-faced gambler opposite him simply shrugged, dropped his hand, and raked in the pot, the chips spilling as he did so.

"Gentlemen," the major announced wearily, "I am temporarily out of funds, but all is not lost, I assure you. If you will excuse me, I'll do what I can to repair my situation."

The other players smiled and nodded at such grandiloquence, and the gambler told the major he was welcome at his table any time. As Major Farber pushed his chair back and got to his feet, another fellow, who had been standing to one side, immediately slipped into the vacated seat, and the game went on.

Slumping down wearily at Agnes's table, the major shook his head and took out his handkerchief. "When Dame Fortune smiles, it is all clover," he told her, mopping his brow, "but when she turns her back on you, it is indeed a cold day in May."

"I brought you bad luck."

He looked quickly at her, immediately concerned he might have hurt her feelings. "Nothing of the kind, Agnes!" he told her hastily. "You are still with me, and the night is young. My luck is bound to change."

Major Farber threw back his shoulders forcefully and looked about him. He brightened considerably, as if by simply uttering such optimism he could indeed transform his luck. But Agnes knew better—through her husband, she had come to know many such men. They played cards the way other men drank—with an obsessive need that bore no relationship to the world about them. She was convinced it was an illness of some kind, though there were many, she knew, who would laugh at such an idea.

She was about to offer the major a small loan to tide him over when the man leaned suddenly forward, eyes alight. "You see," he told her in a hoarse stage whisper, "all is not lost!"

She followed his gaze and saw Jim Mulrey sidling into the saloon. As the small gray man moved to the end of the bar, Agnes shuddered. She could not look upon Mulrey without a feeling of dread. She was as certain as James that it was Jim Mulrey who had fired upon him from the alley beside the Alamo.

"Mulrey owes me close to fifty dollars," the major told her, "and I have it on good authority that he has money. With that business of the stagecoach behind us, we have gotten along decently enough. And just half of what he owes me would put me back into that game. Excuse me, Agnes, while I approach the man."

Before she could say anything to dissuade the major, he was on his feet and heading for Mulrey. Watching anxiously, she saw her friend greet Mulrey and then begin to converse. They seemed to get on well enough, and her apprehension faded somewhat. The two men drank together for a while, chatting amiably. Once or twice she even heard them laughing. Then, with Mulrey leading the way, they left the bar and disappeared into the back alley.

Agnes was worried, but she told herself that the major would not have gone with Mulrey unless he had agreed to pay back the money he owed. Sure enough, after a wait of close to fifteen minutes, she saw the major returning—a mite unsteady on his feet, she thought, but this she attributed to the drinks he had consumed at the bar with Mulrey.

He diligently kept in motion until he reached Agnes's table, but then he lunged rather clumsily for a chair, almost upsetting it as he slumped down. Smiling wanly, he reached out and took Agnes by the hand.

"Thank you for waiting," he told her.

"Did Mulrey pay you what he owed?"

He ignored her question. "Agnes," he asked, his voice weak, "would you be so kind as to help me to my room?"

"Of course," she said, somewhat bewildered.

She helped Major Farber to his feet, and the two left the Pearl with the major leaning somewhat heavily on her arm. She was surprised at the extent of his inebriation, since she did not think he had drunk that much. But then she reminded herself that the drinks he had had with Mulrey were consumed on an empty stomach, since the major had not eaten all afternoon, at least not during that long poker game.

When they reached the major's room on the second floor of the Drovers' Cottage, the man was barely able to walk. It was only with increasing difficulty that she managed to open his door and lead him over to his bed. The moment he reached it, he plunged face down on the fresh quilt, groaning in evident pain.

Agnes hurried back to the door, closed it, then returned to Farber. "What is it?" she asked. "What's wrong, Major?"

When he made no reply, she took him by the shoulder and rolled him over onto his back. As she did so, his swallow-tailed coat fell open, revealing a dark blood stain on his shirt. Startled, Agnes took a step back . . .

and that was when she saw that his trousers were stiff with blood.

Holding her fist to her mouth so as not to cry out, she leaned close to the major. He looked up at her, managing a weak smile.

"Thank you," he faltered. "That was a long walk—a very long walk. I doubt if I could have made it without you."

"Major, who did this?"

"Do not be alarmed," he whispered hoarsely. "It is just a pin prick, I assure you."

"It was Jim Mulrey, wasn't it?"

The major nodded. "It seems the cur did not have the money, after all. But he did have a very sharp dagger. I would be much obliged if you would fetch me a glass of water from the stand over there. I am fearfully thirsty."

Hurrying over to the nightstand, she lifted the pitcher and filled one of the glasses, her hands trembling as she poured. But when she returned to the major, she saw he had passed out completely. Even more disquieting, the blood seemed to have spread over his entire shirtfront.

Alarmed, she put down the glass and ran from the room in search of a doctor.

In the company of deputies Champ Holler and Wilt Coffee, Wild Bill Hickok strode down the center of Texas Street. The saloons and gambling halls were filled to their capacities with rowdy cowpokes, and dance-hall girls were hanging from the upstairs windows, calling down to the passing men. From inside the saloons came the sounds of wild laughter and breaking glass; every now and then a curse, strong enough to burn into a man's memory, could be heard above the din. In the alleys between the buildings, the three men caught glimpses of dance-hall girls taking care of their eager cowboys in a fashion they could not manage on a crowded dance floor. Periodically, cowboys stormed out of the saloons—laughing and hell-raising like the overgrown children they were—mounted their steeds, and galloped drunkenly past Hickok and his deputies.

Hell is really in session tonight, Hickok thought as he cursed the town council for passing that damned ordinance when it had. Against one Texan outfit he and his men might have been able to enforce it, but not against two groups trying to make up for time lost on the trail, with each one trying to outdo the other.

With what came close to being a sense of relief, Hickok heard the first gunshot ring out from a saloon ahead of them. Then came the second shot. By that time Hickok and his deputies, their guns drawn, were running full tilt toward the saloon. A crowd of men convulsing with hilarity burst from the place, with a Texan wearing a sombrero and nothing else firing bullets over their heads as they fled. He obviously was on a spree and meant no harm, but in his condition he was still a menace to life and limb.

By the time the naked cowpoke reached the street, deputy Frank Ames had materialized from the other side of the saloon. As he closed in on the wild man from that direction, Hickok and the other two deputies came at him from the opposite side. Hickok fired two quick shots into the air to gain the cowboy's attention, and stopping instantly, the big, gangling man saw he was surrounded and dropped his weapon, a silly grin on his face.

"Go back in there, someone, and get his clothes!" Hickok barked to the crowd still pouring out of the saloon.

A Texan turned and went back in, and a dance-hall girl started to giggle at the sight of the naked cowboy.

Hickok did not blame her at all; the poor drunken cowpoke looked downright obscene, his white, hairless body glistening in the street lanterns like something that had just crawled out from under a rock. Someone on the other side of the street shouted, "Grab a stick and we'll kill it!"

The huge crowd erupted in laughter just as the fellow who had gone back for the cowpoke's clothes came running out with them. The now subdued and acutely embarrassed roisterer climbed hastily into his britches.

A moment later, as Frank Ames was hauling the partially clothed cowboy off to the lockup, Hickok cleared his throat and in his high, piercing voice called out to the watching crowd to hold up for a minute—he had an announcement to make. The people on the sidewalks grew still.

"I want to remind all of you of that new ordinance," Hickok told the crowd. "Now, we've already had one violation. If anyone else discharges a firearm within city limits, I'm closing down every saloon and dance hall in Abilene."

"You threatening us, Marshal?" someone in back cried. It sounded like Ben Thompson.

"That's not a threat, Ben," Hickok replied. "That's a promise."

There was an audible undercurrent of angry muttering and some cursing, but no one else spoke up, and the sidewalks began to empty as the cowboys and their girls turned back to resume their revelries.

At that point, Hickok saw Mike Williams running up to join them. "I heard the gunshots!" he said breathlessly, reaching Hickok's side.

"Just an inebriated cowpoke," Hickok told him. "How're you feeling?"

"Fine, except for this head," he said ruefully. "I

guess I drank too much, but I feel better now, Bill. I'll survive." He smiled crookedly. "Maybe that's the trouble."

Hickok nodded thoughtfully. "And that's most likely the toughest part of it, Mike—just goin' on like nothing has happened. But people do it every day, and you can, too."

"Hey, Bill, did you mean that—about shutting down Abilene?" Champ Holler asked as the marshal and all four of his deputies continued on down the street.

"I meant it. If things get much wilder, I might not wait for another cowpoke to start blasting. Don't forget, we've got two outfits to contend with, each one trying to outdrink, outgamble, and outwhore the other." He consulted his watch. "Things are wild enough already, and it's only nine o'clock."

"Jesus," said Wilt Coffee. "That's right. It's early yet."

Hickok nodded grimly as he kept on, doing his best to ingore the occasional sound of shattering glass and the shrill cries of liquored-up women as the lawmen passed the saloons along Texas Street.

Sitting with the four Texans who had remained in Abilene to tend to their dying comrade, Phil Coe spent that afternoon and evening nursing himself into a bitter fury. He had decided, after giving the matter much thought, to visit Jess in her room that afternoon. She had been dallying with him long enough; he wanted her to show him how much she loved him.

Her response had been searing. In a tone so scathing it had caused the hair on the back of his neck to rise, Jess had told Coe in no uncertain terms that it was Wild Bill she preferred and no one else. When, stunned and disbelieving, he had haltingly pleaded his love for her, she had laughed scornfully and suggested that even if he were to take a bath and clean his foul mouth, he would still only be good enough for the girls on the other side of the tracks.

Then she had told Coe to get out of her room and never approach her again without an invitation. When he refused to leave, she began throwing things. Ducking awkwardly, Coe fled to the Bull's Head, where straight whiskey with beer chasers had transformed his humiliation into cold, black, unremitting hatred. Unable to believe there could be anything about his person capable of arousing such a repugnance in Jess, he had come to the conclusion that it must have been Wild Bill who had poisoned her against him.

That long-haired gunslinger with the voice of a woman was not content with slapping him around in front of his friends. No, now he wanted Jess back as well.

Sitting around Coe at the table—and just as bitter as he was—the four Texans plied their cohort with more whiskey, goading him carefully, skillfully into revenge against Abilene's marshal.

". . . and we'll back you," said the oldest Texan, a lean fellow with a long scar along one cheek. "You don't have to worry none about that."

His three companions nodded solemnly.

"Hell, I'd need some kind of edge," Coe replied nervously. He had begun to suspect that he was being pushed relentlessly into a corner.

"What kind of an edge?" one of the Texans asked.

"You want me to draw you a picture?" Coe emptied his glass.

"I said, what kind of an edge?"

"Go ahead and tell us, Coe," prompted another.

Coe began to sweat. "Well, that sonofabitch carries two guns, don't forget. And he's got more lives than a cat. You saw what happened when Mulrey tried to bushwhack him from that alley. That man ain't human."

"Oh, he's human. One bullet would take him," a smaller Texan sitting to the left of Coe said. "That's all it would take."

"No," Coe insisted doggedly, reaching for the drink the Texan with the scar had just poured for him. "He's more than that."

"So tell us what you want."

Coe moistened his suddenly dry lips. "You guys would have to back me all the way. And one shot wouldn't be nearly enough."

"Hell," drawled the scarred Texan. "I thought you knew that, Phil. Didn't we just tell you we'd back you?"

Coe was certain of it now: He had backed himself into a corner. "Dammit, talk is cheap. Sure, you say you'll back me, but what's that supposed to mean . . . exactly?"

The man with the scar leaned forward, his cold eyes fixing Coe with a stare that sent ice coursing through his veins. "We each carry a gun. Now, you can count, can't you? That's four guns in all, six shots each. Ain't that enough for you?"

"You mean all five of us go against him?"

"Hell, no. What's the matter with you, Coe? You been drinking our whiskey all this time, but you ain't been payin' no attention to what we been telling you. Is that it?"

"Speak plain. What're you drivin' at?"

"I thought you wanted to kill the sonofabitch so he'd know it was you who done it."

"Well, sure, but . . ."

"Then what are you worried about, Coe? I told you—we'll back you. The sonofabitch won't have a chance."

Before Coe could digest what the Texan was telling

him, Ben Thompson stormed into the saloon, looking so agitated that everyone in the place turned to stare at him.

"What's up, Ben?" someone shouted. "You look about ready to explode."

"It's that damn marshal again!"

"Wild Bill? What's he up to now?"

"The sonofabitch says he's goin' to close us down if one more gun is discharged tonight." Thompson looked over at Coe. "What do you think of that, Coe? The biggest goddamn night we've had in weeks, and he wants to close us down!"

Instantly, Coe saw a chance to get out of the corner these four Texans had painted him into . . . and Hickok was playing right into his hands by making such a threat. All Coe had to do now was arouse these cowboys enough to send them—not Phil Coe—after Hickok's scalp.

He jumped to his feet. "Damn Hickok's hide!" he cried. "How long we goin' to stand for that sonofabitch pushing us around?" Listening to himself, Coe was astonished. He was doing so well, it felt as if someone else—and not he—were speaking.

"So what do you propose, Coe?"

"I say we call his bluff . . . and I say we do it *now!*"

The crowded saloon reverberated with a thunderous cheer. As exuberant hands pummeled his back, Coe strode boldly from the saloon, the four Texans at his side.

Hickok paused on the veranda of the Alamo and took a quick look up and down the street. Abilene was quieting down considerably. In the face of Hickok's ultimatum, some saloons were already shutting their doors for the night. Weary cowboys, their arms wrapped around their girls, were weaving off through the alleys, heading for a place to sleep.

Abilene's three other deputies continued with their rounds, but Mike Williams remained with Hickok. "Seems a mite quieter," Mike observed.

"It does at that. But it's still early yet."

Hickok turned and entered the Alamo, where the night's revelry was still going full tilt. Even the ample-bodied nudes painted on the walls appeared to be taking part in the fun. The click of the roulette wheel and the sound of dice could just be heard above the lively strains of the orchestra.

Shaking his head at those who wanted him to join a poker game, Hickok proceeded to his favorite place at the rear and slumped wearily into a chair, Mike sitting beside him.

A girl hurried over as soon as the two men were seated, and both ordered beer. When the girl returned with their drinks, she told Hickok that Butterfield had something he wanted to tell the marshal, but he was too busy at the bar to visit their table. Hickok and Mike got up and walked over to the bartender.

Butterfield leaned over the bar and spoke softly. "A Mrs. Agnes Thatcher was in here a while ago looking for you, Bill. Seems Jim Mulrey knifed Major Farber."

Hickok frowned. "The major? Damn! How the hell did that happen?"

"She didn't say, Bill, but she's already got a doctor for him. She just wanted you to know what happened. She says the major's in his room at the Drovers'."

"I'll go see what happened," Mike said.

"Get back here as soon as you can," replied Hickok.

Mike hurried from the Alamo, and Hickok went back to his table, his grim expression keeping the other patrons away.

*   *   *

Across the street from the Alamo, Phil Coe slowed to a halt. He was part of a silent but growing crowd made up mostly of sullen Texans who somehow knew what was about to transpire. When Coe saw Mike Williams burst from the saloon, he felt a little easier. With that eager young deputy out of the way, the odds were a little better.

Coe felt more confident with each passing moment. His desperate plan was working perfectly. He had not only the four Texans at his back, but also a growing crowd of surly men, all of them eager to see that long-haired sonofabitch taken down a peg. Turning quickly now for assurance, he saw the four Texans watching him keenly, their six-guns already drawn.

Coe turned back around, stepped out into the street, and started across it for the Alamo. He thought of calling Hickok's name, but the words stuck in his throat. The crowd at his back grew larger, and out of the corner of his eye, he could see dark figures running up to join it. For a moment he felt as though the crowd itself had become a heavy weight pushing on him, impelling him forward.

Stepping up finally in front of the Alamo's veranda, Phil Coe drew his Colt from his belt and swallowed hard. His mouth was suddenly bone dry, and though he wanted to call Hickok out of the saloon, he couldn't.

The next moment a dog, its tail wagging, emerged from the alley beside the saloon. With one glance at the silent, watchful crowd, the mutt put its tail between its legs and started trotting away down the street, its nose to the ground. Coe had an inspiration. Dogs had long been declared a public nuisance in Abilene—Wild Bill was netting fifty cents for every unlicensed dog he shot within the city limits. Well, in this case, Coe would simply save Wild Bill the trouble.

Aiming carefully, Coe shot the dog in the rump, flinging the animal forward onto its back. Rolling over, the wounded dog tried to drag itself away, crying out pitifully in pain. Coe stepped closer and finished the mutt off with another shot, this one to the brain.

Just after the second shot, Wild Bill burst from the Alamo. Coe should have fired on him in that instant— that had been his plan—but a palsy came over him the moment he saw Hickok looming above him on the veranda. Coe lowered his Colt and took a hesitant step back into the crowd.

"That you, Coe?" Hickok demanded from the veranda.

"Yes, it's me, damn you!" Coe replied.

"You the one that discharged that gun?"

"I shot a cur. What's the harm in that? If you want, I'll give you the fifty cents I got coming to me."

"Dammit! I said there'd be no more discharging of firearms tonight! I'll take that sidearm, Coe. Looks like you're goin' to spend the night in the lockup."

While the rest of the crowd continued to shrink back, Hickok swiftly descended the veranda's steps and strode toward Coe.

"Damn you to hell!" Coe cried. "You don't mean you're really going to lock me up!"

"You heard me."

"For shootin' a cur?"

"You know the law, Coe. Let me have that gun."

"Hey, Marshal!" someone in the crowd called. It sounded like Ben Thompson. "You goin' to shut down Abilene now?"

"Damn right I am."

"Over our dead bodies, Marshal," said a tall Texan, stepping from the crowd. A livid scar ran down one cheek.

Turning toward the voice, Hickok recognized the

speaker as the leader of the four men who had remained in Abilene with their dying comrade. The scarred man had a six-gun in his hand, and three other Texans were backing him up.

At once, Hickok realized that Coe's shots had simply been a device to lure him out here for these Texans. It was a trap—and he had walked right into it.

Glimpsing a sudden movement beside him, Hickok turned back to Coe, who was just raising his weapon. Coe fired twice, the bullets tearing harmlessly through the skirts of Hickok's coat. Returning the fire, the marshal caught Coe twice in the stomach, just above the navel, and the force of the slugs flung Coe to the ground. Ducking low, Hickok then swung back to the scar-faced Texan and snapped off a quick shot, but it missed as the Texan ducked swiftly back and fled through the crowd.

As the spectators scattered in panic, Hickok took after his assailant, who had headed down Texas Street toward the depot. But by the time the marshal had made his way through the frightened people in the street, not a glimpse of the scar-faced Texan could be seen. Bringing himself to a halt, Wild Bill, his guns still in his hands, began to turn back. Suddenly a six-gun belched fire from a darkened doorway to his right. As the slug whispered past Hickok's cheek, he saw Jim Mulrey dash from the doorway, a smoking gun in his hand.

Just then he heard another man coming at him from behind! Whirling frantically, Hickok fired once at the onrushing figure, who jerked as the bullet found its mark. But it was not a Texan . . . *it was Mike Williams!*

Mike, his hand clutching at his gut, wore a look of pure surprise. Dropping his gun in dismay, Hickok rushed up to catch the young deputy before he fell, then lowered him gently to the ground.

"My God, Mike. I didn't know it was you."

Mike Williams rolled his glazed-over eyes toward the marshal and spoke haltingly. "Don't feel bad, Bill. . . . It was an accident."

"Where'd I hit you? How bad is it?" Hickok was frantic.

The deputy tried to answer, but he couldn't get it out. As the awed, silent crowd rushed closer to bend over the two men, Mike died in Hickok's arms.

Chapter 11

Less than an hour later, the Kansas moon rose over a shocked, silent Abilene.

Consumed with anguish, Hickok had raged throughout the town immediately after Mike's death, clearing out and closing every saloon, gambling hall, and brothel. A wild, terrible light in his eyes, he dared any Texan, townsman, or saloon owner to object, as if he were seeking someone upon whom he could take out his fury.

Only one irate Texan obliged. Galloping out of town past Hickok, he brandished his revolver threateningly, whooping and yelling out as if to taunt the enraged marshal. Hickok shot the revolver from the Texan's hand, then pounced on the bloody weapon and hurled it after its fleeing owner.

A few moments later, when the proprietor of the Lone Star saloon did not appear to be closing up fast enough, Hickok, with two well-aimed shots, brought down one of his chandeliers and shattered the mirror behind his bar.

Yet even when he had succeeded in shutting down the town, Wild Bill's raging heart could not be quieted. His high voice bellowing eerily, he stalked one more time down Texas Street, calling out to Texans still in

Abilene to clear out. At last he flung himself into the Alamo and sought out his table.

There, in the darkness, a bottle of Maryland rye in his hand, he waited for Jim Mulrey . . . and tried not to think of Mike Williams.

The Alamo door swung open, and Frank Ames and Champ Holler entered nervously. Glancing up at his two deputies, Hickok knew from their wary behavior that even they feared him now—but he did not care.

"Well?" he demanded, pouring himself another shot of rye.

"Coe's in the back of the Bull's Head," Frank said, stepping up nervously to Hickok's table. "He's got two slugs in his gut. He don't like it none, and I guess he's prayin' he'll be gone by morning."

"And Mike?"

"Wilt took him to Skinner's funeral parlor. The old vulture wants to know who's going to pay for the funeral."

"Tell the sonofabitch I am." Hickok looked down at his hands. "Did either of you see Mulrey?"

"No, but we left your message just about everywhere, Bill," Frank said.

Hickok's message was simple enough: Anyone who helped Mulrey escape from Abilene would earn Hickok's lasting enmity, and the only way Mulrey could leave town alive would be to give himself up to Hickok, who would be waiting for him in the Alamo.

"I think Mulrey must have got the message by now," Champ remarked. "Ben Thompson said he would give it to Mulrey personally."

"Who's covering the livery?"

"Wilt."

Nodding, Hickok glared up at both of them. "Don't let that sonofabitch get out of this town. If you do, I'll have both your hides. Is that clear?"

"If we can, Bill, you want us to take him?"

"No. Just be sure to tell him where I am—and what his choices are." When both men nodded, Hickok went on. "Now, what about the major?"

"He'll be all right," said Frank. "That Mrs. Thatcher is with him."

"He swears it was Jim Mulrey, does he?"

"That's right, Bill."

Hickok looked at them for a long, brooding moment. "Thank you, boys. And thank Wilt for me, too, will you?"

"Sure, Bill."

"Now get out of here."

The two deputies wasted no time in doing just that.

The ache within Hickok's breast would not lessen, nor had he any hope it would soon. With bitter irony, he found himself recalling his words to Mike Williams earlier this same fateful evening when he had tried to comfort his young deputy about Sue Ann's death. The toughest thing to do, he had told Mike, was to go on living like nothing had happened.

Now it was Hickok's turn to swallow hard and keep going. He would have to do so, he knew, and do it he would. He knew as well that he could never hope to be entirely free from what he had done this night. Whenever he killed a man, the memory of it would fade away entirely within a few weeks. Then, without warning—during a quiet, reflective moment usually—he would find himself reliving the killing in sharp, numbing detail. It would be the same way with the bitter, needless death of Mike Williams—a young man who had worshiped Wild Bill and who had served him so loyally.

Hickok had no difficulty blaming himself for what had happened. He had panicked and fired too quickly. But just as he realized how his own highly charged state had contributed to the tragedy, he knew also that Jim Mulrey's shot from that doorway had been the final push that had sent Hickok over the edge into panic. If Coe and those four Texans had to share the blame for Mike's death, then so did Jim Mulrey.

Hickok was waiting for Mulrey now in this darkened, shut-down saloon for that very reason. He knew that Mulrey was out there somewhere, prowling through the darkened town, girding himself to meet Hickok's challenge—and meet it he would have to. Hell, how could Mulrey possibly pull back now? Any other options were gone. Furthermore, Mulrey had the advantage of knowing where Hickok was, and it would be Mulrey who would choose the precise moment of attack. To a great extent, the small gray man would control the showdown with the element of surprise. Hickok was just a sitting duck . . . but that thought didn't bother him at all.

Pouring himself another shot of rye, Hickok chuckled meanly to himself. The little sonofabitch might be peering in through a window at that very moment, sizing up the situation.

"Come ahead, you bastard," Hickok muttered as he slung the rye down his throat. "Do your damnedest."

A shadow appeared at the front door. Hickok drew both his guns, then rested them on the table as he saw a familiar figure hurry through the door and move toward him in the gloom. It was Elliot Carson.

"You almost got your head blown off," Hickok told the editor, as Elliot pulled a chair up beside the table and sat down. "What do you want? Another interview? This is a fine time for it."

"I want to talk you out of this madness, Bill," Elliot said. "You've done enough tonight. Abilene is becoming one big graveyard—Coe is dying . . . Mike Williams is dead . . . and that Texan died last night. Now you've sent out a challenge to Jim Mulrey."

"He tried to kill me twice, and he cut up the major."

"I know that, Bill—by now, everyone in Abilene does—but let it go. Get out of here and go on to your room. T. C. Henry and Joe McCoy both asked me to come here. They've given up on Abilene as a trail town. McCoy's going to build another one down the line in Newton. He's finished here, and he knows it. It is time for you to go as well. Abilene belongs to the farmers now, and to those of us who want to rid the town of the vice and violence that caused this night's tragedy."

"This night is not over yet, Elliot. I will thank you to get out of here and let me finish it as I see fit."

"More bloodshed, Bill? . . . Is that what you want?"

"Elliot, you don't understand. I've got to finish this business now . . . tonight. As long as Jim Mulrey remains loose in Abilene, you will have no peace. He's a wild animal. I want him—almost as much as he wants me."

"Is he the only wild animal, Bill?"

Hickok smiled and shrugged. "Have it your way, Elliot. Yes, I am a wild one, too. So let us have at each other, destroy each other perhaps. Then you'll be rid of us both."

"My God, Bill, don't you see how futile all this is—how violence only begets further violence? You shot Jim's brother, and now he must come after you. And those Texans who stood with Coe, will you go after them also? Each one of them? Don't you see? There's no end to it. You'll just go on killing until someone kills you!"

"You don't have the stomach for it, Elliot?"

"I've seen war, Bill—as you have. Under no circumstances could I ever bring myself to kill another human being again—no matter what the provocation." He looked coldly at Hickok. "And I am afraid I have no sympathy for those who can."

"I do not require your sympathy, Elliot. I just want you to get the hell out of here and let me finish my job." ·

Elliot got to his feet. "That's your last word, is it, Bill?"

"You sure as hell take a lot to be convinced. Get out of here, Elliot. A friend I would have welcomed; a preacher I can do without."

Elliot turned on his heels and stalked from the place. From the set of his shoulders, Hickok could tell the man was angry. Too bad, but there was no help for it. Hickok smiled wryly and shook his head. Town marshals shouldn't ever let themselves think they have friends—at least not in the towns they're paid to protect.

"What did he say, Elliot?" Connie asked anxiously as Elliot reached the other side of the street where she was waiting for him.

Outside of Connie and Elliot, Texas Street appeared deserted. Because they were reporters, they felt they had to stand this vigil outside the Alamo; and because Elliot considered Wild Bill his friend, he had risked that friendship in an effort to talk him out of this showdown with Jim Mulrey.

"He told me to get out," Elliot said unhappily. "He called me a preacher, and I dare say I must have sounded like one, at that."

"He wouldn't listen?"

Elliot shook his head sadly. "I just couldn't convince him to quit this deadly game. I'm stumped, Connie, but how can I stand here and let this thing happen?"

169

With a deep sigh, he turned to look back at the darkened saloon. As he did so, he thought he saw a shadowy figure moving across the alley behind the saloon. But when he peered closer, trying to see more clearly, whatever it was had vanished. Perhaps it had just been his imagination . . . or perhaps it hadn't. *Perhaps he had just seen Jim Mulrey.*

He turned to Connie. "Stay here, Connie," he told her softly. "I won't be long."

"Where are you going?"

"I think I saw someone behind the Alamo. I am going in to warn Bill."

"But what shall I do?"

"You're a reporter now. Take good notes." Elliot hurried across the street. In a moment he had reached the alley and disappeared into its black mouth.

Her heart pounding in sudden apprehension, Connie stepped back into a doorway and held her breath, but as she did so, the sound of running footsteps sounded sharply on the wooden sidewalk. Turning, she saw Jess Hazell running toward her.

"I could see you standing here," Jess said, her breathing loud and rapid. "Is Bill still inside the Alamo?"

"I am afraid so."

"Mulrey's gone after him! Ben Thompson just told me."

Then Elliot *had* seen someone!

"Oh, my God," Connie gasped, as her heart began to pound wildly. Elliot was now in this as deeply as Hickok! For the first time Connie realized just how much she cared for Elliot. She cared so much it was hurting her . . . terribly. She glanced at Jess. The girl was hugging herself, eyes wide. At that moment Connie realized Jess was feeling the same kind of anguish that she was experiencing. Reaching out, Connie took Jess's hand in hers and squeezed.

*   *   *

A cold, chilling sweat covered Jim Mulrey, but he did not pause as he turned the knob, pushed open the door, and stepped into the rear of the Alamo. Once inside, he silently closed the door behind him, then waited for his eyes to adjust to the inky darkness.

Mulrey had waited to make his move until Elliot Carson had left the Alamo and reached the other side of the street. He did not want to contend with the reporter's interference, but at the same time Mulrey was glad the man was going to be on hand when he killed Wild Bill. The news would make him famous—and what jury would convict him now? Everyone in Abilene knew it was Wild Bill who had challenged him.

Nevertheless, Mulrey was terrified. When his eyes adjusted to the gloom and he decided to move farther into the Alamo, his feet seemed rooted to the floor. After all, twice before had he attempted to assassinate the man who had killed his brother, and both times he had failed. Now Wild Bill was in here somewhere, waiting for him. Sucking in his breath, Mulrey leaned his back against a wall. His heart was thudding so loudly in his chest, he found it difficult to believe it could not be heard throughout the saloon.

Then he recalled Ben Thompson's betrayal, and bitterness surged through him, giving him strength. Unwilling to brave Wild Bill's fury by giving Mulrey sanctuary, Ben Thompson had demanded that Mulrey leave his place and face up to the marshal. In desperation, Mulrey had turned to his four so-called Texan friends, who were holed up with him. But they, too, had turned their backs on him. Then, when Mulrey had refused to leave, Thompson and the Texans had grabbed him by the scruff of the neck and flung him out into the alley behind the saloon.

171

It was that betrayal which had galvanized Mulrey finally. Struggling to his feet in the lonely darkness of that back alley, he had sworn that not only would he kill Wild Bill, but he would kill Ben Thompson as well.

Recalling that vow, Mulrey's paralyzing fear of Wild Bill eased somewhat. Taking out his six-gun, he pushed himself away from the wall and started to move into the main room of the Alamo. With extreme caution, he placed each foot carefully, putting his full weight on the floorboard slowly . . . gradually . . . before moving on. As a result, he made not a sound as he crept through the darkened saloon. Eventually, his eyes picked out the platform on which the orchestra sat—ahead of him to his right. Directly before him was the end of the long mahogany bar. He stole forward until he reached it, then peered at the tables and chairs along the wall beyond the empty gaming tables.

He thought he saw a dark form sitting at a table near the wall, but he could not be sure. The darkness seemed to pulse as his eyes strained to pierce the maddening gloom. He took one more step to get a closer look, but this time he was not careful.

The board beneath his foot creaked softly, but Mulrey might as well have stepped on the tail of a cat. The figure at the table rose at once. Realizing it was now or never, Mulrey strode toward the man and brought up his six-gun. Both men's guns were fired at almost the same instant, Hickok's twin Colts thundering as they lit up the tables in front of him. Mulrey saw the bottle on Hickok's table shatter just as two powerful, sledging blows struck his own chest, flinging him back against the bar.

Outside in the alley, Elliot Carson froze midstep, cursing in frustration. The thunderous detonations within the saloon told him he was too late. A moment later, fumbling through the gloom toward the back porch, he found the rear door and pulled it open. Hurrying into the building, he foolishly stumbled into a wall and cursed once again.

Abruptly, the gloom ahead of him vanished in a flood of light. Looking into the main room, he saw Jim Mulrey lying face down, a dark pool of blood seeping out from under his body. When Elliot rushed forward to where Mulrey lay, he saw Bill, an oil lamp in his hand, staring down at the sprawled figure.

"My God, Bill! Is he dead?"

Bill had been about to inspect the fallen figure more closely. Looking up at Elliot now, he put the lamp down on the bar and came toward his friend. He seemed genuinely glad to see the editor, and for the first time Elliot got some inkling of what Bill must have been going through as he waited here alone in the darkness for his assassin.

"He should be dead," Bill replied wearily. "I caught him twice. It was a close one, Elliot . . . and he ruined my bottle of rye."

"I thought I saw Mulrey in the alley, and I came to warn you." Elliot shook his head ruefully.

"Thanks anyway. How about a drink?"

Elliot nodded quickly. "Sure, Bill. I think I need one, at that."

The two men turned toward the bar, and that was when Elliot saw Mulrey rise from the floor, a bloody weapon clutched in his hand!

Acting instinctively, Elliot lunged at Bill, flinging him out of the way a second before Mulrey fired. The two men crashed to the floor amidst a clattering wreckage of tables and chairs, one of Bill's revolvers thumping heavily to the floor.

Looking back, Elliot saw Mulrey—eyes wild—looming over them. Propped against a chair, kneeling, he had both hands clutched around his weapon. In that instant, Mulrey's gun thundered again, and the bullet slammed into the floor inches from Elliot's head. Mulrey lost his balance momentarily but then steadied himself. Snatching up Bill's loose gun, Elliot rolled away from the marshal and managed to get off a shot at Mulrey—just as Bill fired also.

As Mulrey crumpled heavily to the floor, Bill jumped up and kicked the fallen man's weapon across the floor. Then the marshal knelt beside him on one knee and, after a quick inspection, glanced over at Elliot.

"He's dead this time."

Elliot got slowly to his feet and handed Bill his weapon. He was a shaken man. When Mulrey had fired on him, he had fired back without hesitation, determined to kill Mulrey before he got the chance to fire upon him a second time. It had happened so quickly he was having difficulty taking it all in.

"Was it . . . was it my shot that killed him?" Elliot managed.

"I'm not sure—but don't let it worry you none," Bill said. "There's a good chance it was my bullet, not yours, that killed him. Your conscience is clean."

"Bill, I made some rather foolish remarks earlier. . . . I know now how it must have sounded to you. You have my apologies."

Bill smiled. "No apology required, Elliot. You said what you believed at the time, and there's no harm in that. Besides, I think you just saved my life."

Elliot nodded wearily and headed for a table. "Maybe I'll take that drink now."

Hickok helped himself to a bottle he found behind the bar and poured them both a drink. They could hear a crowd gathering outside, but neither man paid much attention. All they wanted was to get drunk—very drunk.

Agnes Thatcher was standing to one side of the crowd at the express office with Connie and Elliot. Beside her stood a thinner, somewhat more reserved Major Farber. They were watching as a contingent of townsmen led by Joe McCoy and T. C. Henry bid a fond farewell to Wild Bill Hickok and Jess Hazell, as the two were about to board the stage heading south to Santa Fe.

It made no difference to the departing marshal of Abilene that only a fortnight before, McCoy and Henry had been the town council's leading voices advocating the end of the cattle trade—and the consequent finish of Wild Bill's career here. Bill understood, as did everyone else in Abilene, that an era in the town's violent history was over at last. The town council's vote was only belated recognition of that fact.

The couple's plans were known by almost everyone. With Jess as his manager, Wild Bill was going to stage a buffalo hunt in the East. He would employ real Comanches and real buffalo. There was no doubt in anyone's mind that such a show would be a sensation and that Wild Bill would make a fortune. Already backers from the East were clamoring to join the enterprise.

Wild Bill finished shaking Miles Kramer's hand, excused himself, and hurried over to Agnes and the major. After shaking Major Farber's hand, he smiled, took Agnes's hand in his, and gallantly brushed it with his lips.

"So this is good-bye, is it?" she said.

"I am afraid so," Hickok replied.

"Take care of yourself, James. I understand the East is almost as treacherous as the wild West."

175

Hickok grinned. "That is what I hear, Agnes. Take care of yourself, also. It has been a pleasure knowing you. Perhaps we will meet again."

Agnes smiled archly. "That is my plan, James. Count on it."

Hickok laughed. "All right, I will."

Still smiling, Hickok turned to Elliot and Connie and shook Elliot's hand. The two men had said their good-byes the night before at the Drovers' Cottage after a farewell dinner, with Wild Bill in the company of Jess, and Elliot in the company of his new bride, Connie. But Bill did not want to leave them out now.

"Take care of Connie," he told Elliot. Then he grinned at Connie and said, "And you take care of him."

"That's the plan," Connie told him, blushing.

"Bill!" Jess called. "Hurry!"

Bill turned to see the driver clambering up into his box. With a quick wave, Hickok hurried back, pushed his way through the crowd, and climbed into the stage beside Jess. When the driver cracked his whip and slapped the reins, the stagecoach lurched forward. Through the dust, the well-wishers saw Hickok leaning out, waving.

Agnes waved once, then wiped away a tear. Escorted by the major, she turned and headed back for her hotel.

Watching her go, Connie thought she understood what the older woman was feeling. Then, grateful that the man she loved was not riding out of her life, she hugged Elliot's arm. Smiling down at her, Elliot leaned over and kissed his wife lightly on the forehead. "Let's go to work," he said. "We have a paper to put to bed."

Miles Kramer hurried over to join them, and the

three left together, walking down the street—no longer awash with young cowboys fresh from the trail—past saloons and gambling halls already boarded up.

Hell on wheels had moved down the tracks, and with the departure of Wild Bill Hickok, Abilene's brief moment in the harsh, violent light of history was over.

Epilogue

The incidents beginning with Wild Bill's confrontation with Ben Thompson over the Bull's Head sign and leading to the accidental death of Mike Williams during the shoot-out with Phil Coe—Bill's rival for the affections of Jess Hazell—culminated in Hickok's leaving Abilene in December 1871.

In the summer of 1872, he was in Niagara Falls, New York, where he staged a "Daring Buffalo Chase of the Plains." The buffalo, however, appeared rather sluggish to the audience, and attempting to arouse them, Wild Bill fired a shot into the air. They promptly stampeded, running in frantic circles, with Bill's imported Comanches in hot pursuit. Soon, some stray dogs joined the fun. Several small boys followed the dogs, and then some adults began chasing the boys.

To add to the confusion, the buffalo broke through the wire fence and charged the audience, and someone turned a bear loose. Altogether, it took Hickok and his cowboys several hours to corral the animals. This ended the performance, and when Bill passed the hat, he retrieved a total of one hundred twenty-three dollars and eighty-six cents—not nearly enough to cover the thousands of dollars he had spent to organize the show.

While this ended his "Daring Buffalo Chase," it

did not end his theatrical career. The following year found him on stage in Buffalo Bill Cody's popular play, *Scouts of the Plains*. For the next few years Wild Bill wandered the West, guiding hunting trips or making his living at the gaming tables, and eventually settling down in Cheyenne, Wyoming.

It was in Cheyenne that Agnes Lake Thatcher again caught up with the man she had sworn to marry. And after only a few weeks' courtship, they were married on March 5, 1876. They honeymooned in her hometown of Cincinnati, and a month later Wild Bill left to make a fortune for them both in the Black Hills of Dakota Territory, where gold recently had been discovered. He promised to send for Agnes as soon as their future was secured.

Unlucky at mining, Wild Bill drifted to the gambling tables in one of the new towns that had sprung up almost overnight—a place that already hosted close to twenty-five thousand miners, misfits, madams, and whores. It was the town called Deadwood, where James Butler "Wild Bill" Hickok was destined to play out the final, dramatic chapter of his life . . . a story to be chronicled in the next volume of this series—STAGE-COACH STATION 11: DEADWOOD.

Coming in April, 1984 . . .

FROM THE
CREATORS OF WAGONS WEST

STAGECOACH

STATION 11:

DEADWOOD

HANK MITCHUM

Out of the Black Hills of the Dakota Territory the raw mining town of Deadwood exploded. During the bustling summer of 1876 a brave and colorful troupe of theatrical performers arrives by stage to cash in on the boomtown wealth. Suddenly, they are swept into the deadly drama about to be played out on the streets of Deadwood—side by side with the legendary Westerners, Martha "Calamity Jane" Canary and James "Wild Bill" Hickok.

As ruthless gambling-hall owner Johnny Varnes plots to take control of this rough, teeming town, he finds his schemes obstructed by two tough opponents, stage owner Tom Murdock and Wild Bill. Varnes's simple and vicious solution is to remove both adversaries with a bullet. Trapped in the middle of the battle is the beautiful ingenue of the acting company Ellen Dorsey, whose growing love for Murdock and compassion for the victims of Varnes's brutality leads her to an act of heroism that could prove to be the difference between life and death in Deadwood.

Read DEADWOOD, on sale in April, 1984, wherever Bantam paperbacks are sold.

★ WAGONS WEST ★

A series of unforgettable books that trace the lives of a dauntless band of pioneering men, women, and children as they brave the hazards of an untamed land in their trek across America. This legendary caravan of people forge a new link in the wilderness. They are Americans from the North and the South, alongside immigrants, Blacks, and Indians, who wage fierce daily battles for survival on this uncompromising journey—each to their private destinies as they fulfill their greatest dreams.

**FROM THE PRODUCER OF WAGONS WEST
AND THE KENT FAMILY CHRONICLES—
A SWEEPING SAGA OF WAR AND HEROISM
AT THE BIRTH OF A NATION.**

THE WHITE INDIAN SERIES

Filled with the glory and adventure of the colonization of America, here is the thrilling saga of the new frontier's boldest hero and his family. Renno, born to white parents but raised by Seneca Indians, becomes a leader in both worlds. THE WHITE INDIAN SERIES chronicles the adventures of Renno, his son Ja-gonh, and his grandson Ghonkaba, from the colonies to Canada, from the South to the turbulent West. Through their struggles to tame a savage continent and their encounters with the powerful men and passionate women in the early battles for America, we witness the events that shaped our future and forged our great heritage.

☐ 22714	White Indian #1	$3.50
☐ 22715	The Renegade #2	$3.50
☐ 22716	War Chief #3	$3.50
☐ 22717	The Sachem #4	$3.50
☐ 22718	Renno #5	$3.50
☐ 20559	Tomahawk #6	$3.50
☐ 23022	War Cry #7	$3.50
☐ 23576	Ambush #8	$3.50

Prices and availability subject to change without notice.

TALES OF BOLD ADVENTURE AND PASSIONATE ROMANCE FROM THE PRODUCER OF WAGONS WEST

A SAGA OF THE SOUTHWEST
by Leigh Franklin James

The American Southwest in the early 19th century, a turbulent land ravaged by fortune seekers and marked by the legacy of European aristocracy, is the setting for this series of thrilling and memorable novels. You will meet a group of bold, headstrong people who come to carve a lasting place in the untamed wilderness.

☐ 23170 Hawk and the Dove #1 $3.50
☐ 23171 Wings of the Hawk #2 $3.50
☐ 20096 Revenge of the Hawk #3 $3.25
☐ 22578 Flight of The Hawk #4 $3.50
☐ 23482 Night of The Hawk #5 $3.50

Prices and availability subject to change without notice.